THE THIEVES

A HIGH-STAKES ENTERTAINING THRILLER

SUSAN SPECHT ORAM

SOS COMMUNICATIONS LLC

THE THIEVES

A high-stakes entertaining thriller

SUSAN SPECHT ORAM

SOS Communications LLC

Published by SOS Communications LLC in 2023

www.susanspechtoram.com

First Edition

Cover design by Best Page Forward

ISBN: 979-8-9870410-2-4 (paperback)

ISBN: 979-8-9870410-3-1(e-book)

✳ Created with Vellum

AMATEUR HOUR

Bets was driving when a flash of light coming from a sprawling one-story building on the outskirts of town struck her as odd. She pulled over and killed the lights.

"Why'd you stop?" Zerk said. "We're going to the apartment, watching a movie."

The car smelled like burgers, fish and French fries.

"We may need to change plans." She pointed. "There's a good chance a robbery's going on over there. Take a look, and tell me what you think."

Zerk pulled his double-patty bacon cheeseburger from a Roy's Best Burgers white sack. He took a bite and hunched over, training his eyes on the commercial laundry.

Bets grabbed her fish sandwich and chomped down. Skin on her arms pricked with goosebumps. This could be the big one and could change their lives.

A young woman in her early thirties and a man about the same age hauled trash bags out a side door. They threw them in the back of a car and glanced around before ducking back inside. If anyone had ever looked guilty, it was these two.

"I see what you mean," Zerk said. "Amateur hour. Obvious as heck."

She chuckled. "Might as well put up a sign saying Robbery in Progress." She rummaged in a bag. "Did you get extra tartar sauce like I asked?"

Mimi, their little white dog, sniffed the air and yipped.

"Sorry, hon, I forgot. Next time, I'll remember."

She nodded but knew better. Her husband was a sweet talker, but following through wasn't his greatest strength. "We'd better check out what's in that car. Are you thinking what I am? Use the usual approach?"

He licked his fingers. "We'll slap the beacon strobe light you bought me for my birthday on the rooftop and pull them over, impersonate police officers and take the loot. Whatever's in that car, I'm pretty sure it's not dirty laundry. But it could be laundered money." He rubbed his hands together.

She smiled. "Points to me for packing to-go bags in the car."

"You're always ready for a robbery." He patted her shoulder.

She punched the air. "We'll seize the opportunity."

"If the haul's big enough, we'll leave our old life behind and never go back to the dumpy apartment."

"There they are now," she said in a hushed voice.

The young couple came out of the building, glanced around and hopped in a car.

Bets dropped her fish sandwich in the sack and started the engine.

"Watch out kids, here we come."

1

JAS

Jasmine Bucker and Phil Reisner threw trash bags in the back of Phil's Toyota hatchback and hopped in the car. Her heart thumped. They'd just stolen more than five-hundred-thousand dollars from the commercial laundry on the outskirts of Las Vegas where she worked as an accountant.

It was ten at night, when her boss always played poker in the back of a pool hall.

Phil went the speed limit, heading out of town on a two-lane blacktop road.

Jas smiled. Part of the money would pay for her father's life-saving treatment.

"We did it," she said.

Ripping off her disposable gloves, she tossed them out the window. Their first and last robbery was over, signed and sealed, a success. Check that off the to do list.

A car came up behind them. A red and blue roof light came on. A siren went off.

A woman's amplified voice said, "Pull over. I repeat, pull over."

"All I did was throw out my gloves," Jas said with a shrug.

Phil kept his eyes on the road, driving with his hands at ten and two o'clock as though he was in a driver's education class and hadn't heard the order.

"This is the police. Pull over immediately."

A dog barked in the background.

Jas wiped her brow. "We can't be stopped, not with the money in the back."

"If we get arrested, you owe me," he said in a shaky voice.

"I'm sorry I dragged you into this."

Phil put on his blinker and pulled off to the side of the road.

"I wanted to help you help your dad," he said, reaching for her hand. "We'll get through this."

Squeezing his warm fingers, Jas regretted dragging her friend into this. She counted to fifty and repeated the exercise.

A woman and a man stepped out of a car and strode over. They wore black suits and mirrored sunglasses. The woman knocked on the driver's side window.

"Open your windows and hand that man your identification."

The man knocked on the window glass. "Ma'am? Will you roll this down? We need to talk with you."

She let go of Phil's hand and rolled down the window.

"Your IDs?" the man said, adjusting his mirrored sunglasses.

Jas eyed the dragon tattoo high on his neck, peeking out from under a black turtleneck. She could make out the eyes, head, and claws. A turtleneck didn't seem like something an officer would wear. Maybe they were undercover cops in an unmarked vehicle.

She handed him her driver's license.

"You too." The woman had blond bobbed hair with bangs. It looked like a wig. On the right side of her nose was a black mole.

Phil passed his driver's license to Jas to give to the dark-haired man.

"While my partner runs those through the system," the woman said, "I need you to open the back of the car."

Jas cringed. They couldn't open the trunk. If they did, they'd be found out.

"Why aren't you wearing uniforms?" Jas said. "And where are your badges? We're not opening the back unless you show us identification."

"Good call," Phil said in a low voice.

The blond officer said, "Get out of the car and put your hands over your heads."

Phil said, "We've done nothing wrong."

"We saw you litter. We'll issue a ticket, but we need to see what's in the trunk."

Beads of sweat glistened on Phil's forehead. "I can't, the latch is broken."

The woman cocked her head. "If we have to, we'll break the back window to get in. We were given orders to inspect this vehicle."

"What if we offered you money to let us go?" Jas said. "We'll drive away and never mention this to anyone." She bent to pick up her purse.

"Drop it," the blond said. "Get out of the car now, hands in the air."

Jas looked at her good friend. She'd talked him into this

scheme. She'd told him after paying for her father's medical care, they'd have enough money left over to drop out of the 24/7 work that wore them down.

A gun hammer cocked.

Jas gasped.

The woman said, "I repeat, get out of the car. Hands up and lean against the car."

Jas said, "We'd better do what she says." She got out on shaky legs.

When they put their hands in the air, a dog barked. She turned her head. A little white dog was in the front passenger seat of the unmarked police car.

Cops didn't drive around with little dogs. She tried to make out the license plate. Nevada. ZRK something.

The man handcuffed her wrists in front of her. She smelled garlic on his breath.

"Garlic for dinner?" she said.

He tilted his head. "Szechwan chicken for lunch. Good nose."

The woman handcuffed Phil, with his hands in back.

"Lean against the side of the car," the man said, "while we inspect your vehicle. Pop the trunk, Bets."

The woman went around back. When she pushed a button, the trunk lid went up.

Jas bit her lip.

"What do we have here?" the blond said. "Black plastic bags." She opened one. "Sweetie, we hit the jackpot. These are filled with cash."

She lifted one. "We'd better take them for inspection at the station, don't you think, Zerk?"

"That's private property," Jas said. "You can't do that."

Bets smiled. "Not anymore. We're taking these off your hands."

Phil said, "Leave us alone, and we'll pay you."

Zerk shook his head. "No deals. You made the mistake of being amateurs."

Jas shivered in the cool desert night air. Her father was counting on getting the money soon. She'd promised him.

While Bets trained a gun on them, her partner picked up a bag and took it to their car.

Jas said, "Please, just take one bag. Leave the rest for us. What's in those bags is important to my family."

Zerk carried the rest of the bags to his car, ignoring her pleas. "Got it all."

Bets said, "Did you check behind the front seats?"

"Yep, you bet, honey bun." The man opened the hood and yanked out a part. "Got the distributor. That'll take a while to fix. Get their cell phones, and let's go."

Bets plucked a cell from Phil's pocket. Leaning in the car, she took a phone from Jas's purse. "I have both cell phones."

When her knees went weak, Jas leaned against the car for support. She'd planned an easy caper for two first-time criminals. But the risks of getting caught were greater than she'd estimated. She'd failed her father.

"Take the cuffs off, and let's go," Zerk said, heading to their sedan.

Bets laughed. "Let's leave them as they are. They'll never find us."

As the two drove off, the horn honked, making Jas jump.

Bets cackled. "Have fun, you two. Next time, leave it to the professionals."

The car raced down the road.

Phil said, "What just happened?"

Jas shuddered. "The robbers got robbed. My boss will figure out I stole his money, because I had the combination to the safe, and I won't be at work tomorrow. We need to find those two and get it back. My dad will die if I don't help him."

She yanked on the handcuffs but couldn't get them off.

"I'll track them down if it's the last thing I do."

2

BETS

Betsy Ringer hooted as they drove off, leaving the empty-handed robbers stranded by the roadside.

"Watch them try to get out of that," she said, nudging her husband, Mark Zerkowitz. "We're going where they'll never find us."

"We shouldn't have used our nicknames in front of them. They might piece it together and figure out who we are, track us down."

Bets laughed and pulled off her blond wig, tossing it out the window.

"We'll be fine. We'll move to a small town and blend in. We won't flash our money around."

She looked him over. "But you've got to get that neck tattoo removed. The dragon is too obvious. You can't wear turtlenecks in the summer. It'll look suspicious. Weren't you supposed to get it taken off last week?"

Driving, he kept his eyes on the road and shrugged. "Something came up."

The way he was acting set off an inner alarm. What if they got to a town, and he mentioned how they're sitting on a load of stolen cash? He'd been known to blab, like when he mentioned to her best friend Cassie they were working on a secret project, and she might not hear from them in a while. Word got out about their planned museum heist, and it fell apart. Talk about poor judgement.

"What came up?" she said. "You never said."

"Dentist appointment."

She swatted his arm. "I don't believe you. You'll have to do better than that."

"I don't have to tell you everywhere I go. You're not my boss."

"Well, I am now. I set up this operation, pretending we're cops. From now on, tell me who you talk to and what you've said. Don't go out for a beer and brag."

He groaned. "We're going to paradise and taking on new identities. You're making it like a prison, with me reporting in. You've got to learn to relax and trust me."

She bit the inside of her cheek, wondering how she was going to spend the rest of her life hidden in a small town with this idiot she couldn't stop loving.

"Pretty hard to do after you told Cassie we were up to something before our last job. There's the turn-off to I-5. Go north and keep on going. I'll drive in a few hours."

He turned the radio to a classical music station. "Driver picks the music."

Bets gritted her teeth. She preferred talk radio. "Long drive ahead of us."

3

JAS

Jas ran to the middle of the two-lane road and waited for a car to come by. Her hands shook. They were stranded.

What were the thieves' names? Bet and Zerks? No, that wasn't it. Bets and Zerk was more like it. When she got out of these handcuffs, she'd look them up online to see if anyone looked like them.

Phil came over and stood by her, hands cuffed behind his back. "This is not the rosy picture you painted when you told me your plan."

She frowned. "Turns out I'm a failure as a robber. I shouldn't have thrown the gloves out the window."

"I think they spotted us earlier."

"Yeah, that's the way they acted." She scuffed her sandaled feet.

"Why'd you pick me? You could've asked someone else to help you."

She smiled. "I needed your computer skills and your car. And you're a good guy."

He brightened. "I was fast at disabling the security cameras."

"You're a genius. I'll have my dad send you chocolate if we go to prison."

He shuddered. "I signed up to give your dad a chance at living, not to get locked up for the rest of my life."

A car approached.

Squinting into the oncoming headlights, Jas held up her handcuffed hands.

"Help."

"Help us," Phil yelled.

When the car roared toward them. Jas broke into a sweat. She and Phil skittered over to car, breathing hard.

She screamed, "Stop."

The car slowed. The windows rolled down.

Jas said, "They're going to help us."

A man said, "I almost hit you. Stay off the road."

"Our car broke down, and we were robbed," Phil said, struggling to free his hands from behind his back.

"Call the cops."

"They took our phones." She held up her bound hands. "We're handcuffed."

"Good luck. I don't want to get involved."

The man closed the windows and sped out of sight.

Jas said, "I'll pull out the tarp and leave it on the road. Maybe that'll make someone stop."

She opened the trunk and tugged at the tarp. Metal cuffs cut into her wrists. This wasn't the trip she'd envisioned, loaded with cash and laughing all the way to her dad's.

Phil said, "Car's coming."

She dumped the tarp on the road and ran back to Phil, panting from the effort.

A car with high beams on slowed and pulled in behind them.

A police officer got out.

Jas said, "Let me do the talking."

"Fine with me."

"Good evening," the officer said, stopping six feet away. "What've we got here?"

Jas said, "I'd like to see your badge."

He flashed a badge and put it away. "Describe what happened."

"We were out for a romantic drive, isn't that right, sweetie?" She looked to Phil for confirmation.

Phil nodded. "That's right, and I was going to propose. But two people stopped us, disabled our car and put us in handcuffs."

Jas said, "They pretended to be cops."

"They took the distributor," Phil said. "Can you remove these handcuffs?"

The officer studied the situation. "I got a call about two handcuffed people stopping people and posing a danger to passersby. Were they dressed as police officers?"

Jas shook her head. "No."

"Did they show you badges? What gave you the impression they were officers of the law?"

Phil said, "They had a light on top of their car, and they aimed a gun at us."

"What do you think they were after? Any idea? Or was this some kind of prank?"

Sweat trickled from her armpits down her arms. "I'm not sure."

The officer said, "What did they take?"

If he learned about the money in the trunk, they'd be

hauled off to jail. While she was behind bars, her dad would die. She had to hunt down the cash and save her father's life.

"Our cell phones," Phil said, moving his shoulders. "And our drivers licenses. Would you please uncuff us?"

"What'd they look like? Did they address each other by name?"

Jas fiddled with her fingers. She'd never get the money back if the police tracked the thieves down. She'd opened the walk-in safe and taken the risk. The money was hers.

"They didn't use names," she said, glancing at Phil. "The woman had long red hair. He was blond. They wore designer glasses and looked like they were in their twenties, don't you think?"

Phil nodded. "Maybe in their late teens."

She smiled at Phil for his quick thinking, lowering the age range that much. Now the cops wouldn't know the thieves were in their late thirties.

"Officer, would you please uncuff us?" she said, holding out her wrists.

"Before I unlock the cuffs, I'll take your IDs and run them through the system."

Phil grimaced. "That's what those two said, then they took off with our driver's licenses. We don't have ID."

"I'll need you to come down to the station and file a complaint."

Her pulse raced. They couldn't go to the station. The police would realize she worked at the laundry that was robbed. She'd be accused of hightailing it out of town.

"It must've been a crazy prank," she said. "We'll be on our way if you uncuff us and call a tow truck."

The officer nodded. "You say they were in their late teens to early twenties? She was a redhead, and he was blond?"

Phil said, "That's right."

"What color were their glasses?" the officer said.

She shrugged. "Hers were turquoise. His were red."

The officer jotted down notes. "I'll take your license plate number just in case."

Jas gulped. They'd have to ditch the car now and steal another one. Anything that could be traced to them, they'd have to leave behind.

"And your names?" the officer said.

"Letitia Babbidge and Charles Fox," Jas said, giving Phil a quick side look.

He wrote those down and opened the handcuffs. A call came in over the police officer's radio about an injury accident.

"I've gotta leave, but I'll call a tow truck," he said.

"Thanks," Jas said, rubbing her wrists.

They needed a getaway car, but she had no idea where to find one. She'd talk with Phil to see what he thought. He was the rational one, the genius brain. Together, they'd get out of this mess.

4

BETS

Bets looked at the phone she'd taken from Jas and checked the news. Better to use someone else's data plan than her own and rack up higher charges. Nothing yet about the robbery, so that was good. She searched online for the best small towns to move to as their little dog, Mimi, settled on her lap.

"Okay, I was thinking of a place called Gold Beach to hide out," she said, turning down the volume on a Mozart symphony that was giving her a headache. "It's a little town on the Oregon Coast."

"Elevation?" Zerk said.

She screwed up her face. "What kind of question is that? Elevation?"

"Tsunamis, earthquakes, you never know." He glanced over. "Look it up."

Scrolling through pages online, she found the information. "Fifty feet."

"Nope, we're not moving there. I'd rather not be stuck in a tiny town anyway. We'd be in danger of being swept away in a tidal wave. Couldn't get to high ground fast enough, if there is any in the area. Not the way I want to die."

"You've thought about this pretty hard, haven't you? How would you like to die? Do you have an idea in mind you'd like to share with me, your dear wife?"

"Not by fire, not by carbon monoxide poisoning, not by rat poisoning, that'd be painful and drawn out. Just a quick whack in the back of the head, and I'll be out cold."

She nodded. "Quick and easy, eh? No mess, just wham, by surprise?"

"Yep."

"I'll remember that, but I want to go out at the same time as you. We're a matched pair, especially after pulling off that highway stop and taking their money." She smiled at him. "We can't ever split up. We have to stick together and keep each other's secrets."

He chuckled. "Trapped in my lover's arms. I can do that."

She went back to Jas's phone. Best small towns to live in the Pacific Northwest, where they'd disappear into the rain, and no one would look for them.

"How's this? Millersville, Washington. Eighteen thousand people, a scenic town seventy feet above sea level and a perfect place to hide from the authorities."

"Where is it?" he said, turning the radio volume up as he drove.

"North of Seattle about two hours. Near some islands."

"Sounds like a good place to try. How long until we get there?"

"Seventeen more hours, depending on traffic," she said. The dog barked. "We'll need to stop at a motel that takes dogs. I'll look for one online."

5
____

JAS

While they waited for a tow truck, Jas and Phil worked on a plan to follow the robbers and recover the money.

"I'll track the location of our phones with my laptop," Phil said. "I can monitor what they're looking up on the internet, if they use our phones."

"Glad you know what you're doing," she said, plunking into the driver's seat.

In the passenger seat, he opened his laptop and pushed a button on a black rectangular handheld device.

"What's that?" she said. "It's cute."

"My Verizon Jetpack, a mobile hotspot for my laptop's wireless connection. Three bars, that's good. Here we go." He typed. "The thieves searched for best small towns to live in. They looked at a place on the Oregon Coast."

Jas nodded. "That's where we go next. But we need a different car so the police can't trace us."

A tow truck pulled up and parked in front of the car.

Phil stowed his devices in his backpack, and they got out.

A tall block of a man in brown coveralls climbed out of the truck.

"I'm Dan, your tow truck driver."

Jas said, "Nice to meet you, Dan. We need a tow, and then we have to switch to a different car."

Phil said, "We were robbed. We're pretty shaken up."

He slung an arm over her shoulder. Presenting a united front, she pretended like they'd done this a hundred times before. She leaned into his warmth in the cool night air.

Dan cocked his head. "What's wrong with driving this car after it's fixed?"

"We can't wait for it to be fixed," Jas said. "We've got to be somewhere, and it wasn't running very well anyway. It probably wouldn't have gotten us to the coast."

"What'd the thieves take?" Dan said.

Phil said, "The distributor."

"And some sneakers and his golf clubs," Jas said.

Phil gave her an odd look.

"Phil's a pro golfer," she said, "so his clubs mean a lot to him. When we get a different car, we'll be on our way. He needs to get to a golf tournament."

Dan's eyes grew wide. "Are you Phil Mickelson, the famous golfer?"

Phil shrugged. "I'm going undercover so no one will recognize me."

"We're going to that famous golf course in Oregon," Jas said. "I forget the name."

"Ocean Dunes Golf Resort," Dan said, snapping his fingers. "Always wanted to go there. Tell you what, we'll go together."

"Pardon me?" Jas said. She must have heard him wrong.

Phil raised his eyebrows. "I don't need another caddy."

Dan said, "Either the three of us are going to Oregon, or

we'll go to my place in the desert, and you'll meet my mother. Which'll it be?"

Jas and Phil crossed their arms and looked at each other.

She whispered to Phil, "We don't have much choice. We're stuck out here. We need to get going."

Dan's phone rang and he pulled it from his pocket. "Mom? I just met some very nice people. I think you'll like them."

Jas heard a woman's shrill voice say something.

Dan shoved the phone into her hand. "She wants to talk with you."

Clearing her throat, Jas said, "Hello?"

"I can't wait to meet you. The last two people staying with us left in a hurry."

Jas whooshed out a breath. The odd invitation out of the blue was suspicious, reminding her of a psycho movie. They couldn't get sidetracked by going to Dan's place and getting sucked into a strange abyss. She'd promised to take her dad to an experimental medical center in a few days.

"Your son is taking us to the Oregon Coast," Jas said. "It'll give him a break for a few days."

Dan took the phone. "I'll see you in a week. I'm going with my new friends. Yes, I'll take my jacket. Love you, bye."

Dan hung up. "Well, that's decided. We'll leave your car. My mom will come out with our other truck and get it. Now let's get started with our vacation. What's your name, dear?"

Jas swallowed hard. "Jas."

"Jas and Phil, let's go to Ocean Dunes, so Phil can golf. Are you ready?"

His deep, booming laugh made Jas crack a smile. He sounded like he was enjoying life. Either that, or he was unstable. She crossed her fingers and hoped they'd be safe with him.

"You've got a professional driver," Dan said, "with a big rig to deliver you to the match. But you'll have to pay for gas."

Phil said. "Could your mom sell my car, and we'll use the money to pay for gas?"

"Sure," Dan said. "Little lady, you get the middle seat. You'll be a Jas sandwich." He chuckled.

Jas said, "I'll get my purse and some other things from the car."

"Me too," Phil said.

"Leave the key under the driver's seat for my mother," Dan said. "She'll take care of your car."

Jas took her purse and messenger bag with her laptop. Phil grabbed his backpack.

"I should've brought a change of clothes," she whispered. "I'm not a very good thief."

He raised his eyebrows. "Clothes are the least of our problems."

They climbed in the truck and, as Dan drove off, Jas spotted the blond wig.

"Please, go back," she said. "I want to get that wig on the roadside."

Dan stopped and backed up. "I just want to say, I'm not into threesomes or handcuffs. I'm more of a traditional guy, if you know what I mean."

"Neither are we," Phil blurted out.

Jas rolled her eyes. She and Phil were platonic friends. At this point, they'd veered so far from her original plan, they might as well be in North Dakota.

Getting out and fetching the blond wig, Jas bounced it against her leg to shake off dust and dirt. She'd wear it when she stole her father's cash back. The thieves who robbed them would be empty-handed by the time she was finished with them.

6
___

BETS

Forty minutes later, Bets pointed to a freeway sign for a rest area. "Let's pull over there. Mimi needs a potty break, and I do too."

"One of us has to be by the car at all times," Zerk said, "to guard the money."

The rest area was a buzzing mini-city at night, with street lights glowing and most of the parking spaces filled with RVs, camper vans, and cars. Semitrucks parked nearby, some with engines running.

After Bets came back, Zerk used the restroom.

She walked the dog in a graveled area and ignored posted signs saying, "No pets in this area."

Rules didn't apply to her or Zerk. They could do whatever they liked, including stealing money from the nice young couple tonight. She smiled, looking forward to talking with Zerk about building a house when they settled in a town. It'd be a house built into a hill with few windows for burglars to climb through.

This was the big one they'd always talked about. Check that box and move on to living the good life.

A police officer on foot slowed and peered in their car windows.

Bets picked up her little dog and hurried over. "Can I help you? This is my car."

Mimi growled and barked.

The man showed his badge.

"Just checking. We're on the lookout for stolen property."

"Well, we sure don't have it. We're on a family vacation, aren't we, dear?" Bets turned to Zerk, who was striding over to them, his lips forming a thin line.

"That's right," he said, putting his arm around his wife's shoulders. "We're finally taking time to see the country."

"Can't wait to see Yellowstone," Bets said, smiling as wide as she could. Her heart was beating like a drum. If only the officer would move on and leave them alone. "I hope I'll get a photo of a bear on top of a car."

"You just might," the officer said. "Have a good trip."

Bets handed the dog to Zerk. "I'll drive."

She climbed in the driver's seat and started the engine. "Let's get out of here."

In the passenger seat, Zerk yawned.

"I'm too old for this. How about you drive another hour, and we'll find a motel? I'm beat."

An hour later, Bets parked and paid for a Super 9 pet-friendly motel room with a view of the parking lot, train tracks and the freeway. Her eyes smarted from cleaning solvents. The threadbare carpet was damp from being shampooed. It was the last room they had left.

"Ninety bucks a night for this?" she said to Zerk as he came in.

She opened the door to the hall to air the place out.

A large man with a gray mustache, twinkling blue eyes

and white suspenders with the words "Lumberjack" in black letters came by with a small dog on a leash.

"Nice evening," he said.

His dog barked.

Mimi ran out and sniffed the other dog.

"Hope we won't bother you," the lumberjack said. "We're next door."

"I'm sure you won't," Bets said. She scooped up Mimi. "Goodnight."

She and Zerk planned to sleep in shifts to protect their car, which was parked near the room in full view of the window. Zerk was standing there now, jingling change in his pockets as he stared at the dimly lit lot.

She closed and locked the door. She was too tired to drive, but not as fatigued as Zerk.

"Why don't you take the first shift sleeping?" she said. "I'll wake you in three hours."

"Thanks."

Zerk brushed his teeth and went to bed with a sigh while Bets settled in an easy chair. She went to Jas's Netflix account on the phone and watched her favorite movie, "Ocean's Eleven." Every now and then she'd glance out the window to be sure no one was near their car.

Car doors slammed, and she looked up. A car had parked next to theirs, and a man and a woman walked toward the lobby. Someone knocked on the room next door.

The lumberjack said, "Who is it?"

"Alicia and Ron."

"Come in," the lumberjack said as his dog barked.

It was an unusual time of night to visit.

Mimi whined and paced in the room.

Thirty minutes later, the lumberjack's door opened. People said goodbye in loud voices and went down the hall. The lumberjack's dog barked, and his door slammed shut.

Mimi yipped.

"Shhh," Bets said as her dog pawed at the door.

"What is it?" Zerk said in a sleepy voice.

"Nothing, go back to sleep."

Bets turned to look out the window.

The man and woman hurried to their car, got in and drove away.

A few minutes later, a car pulled in and parked in the same spot. A man stumbled out and went into the lobby. Someone knocked on the lumberjack's door. The door opened, and the lumberjack's dog barked. When the door closed with a thump, Mimi barked.

Twenty minutes later, the door slammed.

Bets stood at the window, keeping an eye on her car, until the man drove off.

She glanced at Zerk, who was snoring despite the commotion. A car pulled up. Soon, it sounded like a party was going on next door.

Twenty minutes later, a woman left.

Bets frowned. The lumberjack must be selling drugs. The activity next door could bring the police to the motel, and their car would be searched.

A man ran into the motel and pounded on the lumberjack's door, making the dog next door bark. Mimi yapped. Bets picked her dog up.

She paused the movie and sighed. By tomorrow night, they'd be in their new hometown. Bets checked the car and put her ear to the wall. All she could hear was low voices. The door opened.

A man said in a loud voice, "Don't sell in my territory or else."

Bets raised her eyebrows.

The door slammed, the dogs barked, and Bets picked up Mimi, taking her over to the window.

A man opened his car door and looked around. He pulled a hammer from his car and smashed the glass in Bets and Zerk's rear passenger window.

"Don't mess with my territory," he shouted.

Bets shook her fist. "It's my car, you fool."

The man hopped into his car and peeled out of the parking lot.

She hurried to the bed and pushed on Zerk's shoulder.

"Wake up. Someone broke our car window."

He opened his eyes, jumped out of bed and pulled on his clothes.

"Did they take anything?"

"No, I caught them in the act. A dealer told the guy next door to stay out of his turf. Then he smashed our window."

Zerk said, "We've gotta get out of here. This is way too much heat for us."

They hurried out to their car.

Driving off, she said, "This is my last night at a budget motel. From now on, it's first class all the way."

"You bet, no more budget hotels for us. We're better than that now."

7

JAS

As the truck rumbled along, Jas used the time to map out what she and Phil, who was asleep, had to do next. Adrenaline kicked in, and she squirmed in her seat. There was no way she could close her eyes, jammed between the two men.

Dan burped. The air in the cab smelled like Cheetos.

She waved a hand in front of her face.

"Pardon me." Dan hummed a tune. "How far to Ocean Dunes?"

"If I can borrow your phone, I'll look it up," Jas said. "We'll take the fastest route."

"I wanted to take the scenic route," Dan said, sounding sad. He fished in his jacket pocket and handed her a phone.

Without a password or facial recognition, it would be easy to steal this device. And she would when she found the opportunity. She'd turned into a crook. Now nothing mattered but her dad.

Straight-laced and a rule follower, she wasn't one to speed. She balanced her checking account every Sunday. Everything changed the day she got the call.

"Jasmine," her father had said in a wavering voice. "I've got news, and it's not good. Are you sitting down?"

Her pulse quickened as she closed the door to her office, sank into a chair and stared at the parking lot. "I'm sitting. Go ahead. Tell me what happened."

"You know I've had that cough? The doctor says I've got a rare lung disease. I might have six months left to live."

Tears streamed down her cheeks. "I'll look into it. We'll get you cured. There has to be something that'll help you."

After that, she'd talked to experts and found the clinic outside Tijuana, Mexico.

Now, she frowned. Instead of sitting in a tow truck, she should be with her dad and taking him to the treatment center.

She said to Dan, "Phil has to get to his golf tournament. After we split up, you can go home the scenic route."

"But we're like family now. We're a triple-pack. I want you to meet my mother."

"We'll separate when we check in at the hotel," she said in a firm voice.

"We'll stay in one room, and you'll go back with me. You'll like my mother."

"I need to be clear about this," she said. "We're taking separate rooms. And we won't go home with you. We have lives of our own and a task we must accomplish."

"My feelings are hurt," he said. "You don't want to be around me."

This was a delicate time, and Phil was deep asleep. She had to handle it without hurting the big man's feelings. They couldn't stick with him forever. They had to follow the trail of the thieves before it went cold.

"I'm sure you're a fine person to be around. I just need privacy."

"You don't want to be near me," he said. "I get the message."

He pulled out a handkerchief and blew his nose.

She shook her head. A big man with a tow truck wanted to be their friend and take them home to meet his mother. If I can make it until tomorrow and be free of this tender-hearted, possibly unstable man, she told herself, I'll donate to a children's hospital and volunteer in my spare time.

Next to her, Phil snorted in his sleep.

Dan said, "If you don't promise to share a hotel room, I'll leave you by the side of the road. I'll take Phil's backpack and your bag. You'll have nothing. How'd you like that?"

Her hands turned cold. She picked up Dan's phone and turned toward Phil, texting her friend Cass where they were and asking for help.

"Come get us," she wrote.

When she hit send, nothing happened.

Cell service not available.

Deep in the woods, they headed for the coast. Wisps of fog blew past. She hadn't seen another car for miles. An isolated two-lane road was not where she wanted to be dropped off in the dark.

He took his foot off the accelerator and glanced at her. "How about here?"

She swallowed. The next town was forty or more miles away. If Dan dropped them off, they'd be stuck trying to track down the thieves without transportation or their laptops. It could take a day to hitch a ride, and who knows where that would take them. They could be murdered by a stranger taking them into the forest.

She let out a slow, calming breath. Her imagination was getting away from her. They couldn't be left by the side of the road. It carried too many risks.

If only she'd foreseen this event when she planned the robbery. But she couldn't have. It was surreal, sitting boxed in between two men, riding in a tow truck with a man named Dan who had a soft spot for his mom and wanted to share a hotel room. She was desperate to help her dad, but she drew the line at a group grope.

For weeks, she'd watched when her boss opened the safe and noted where he kept the combination. She'd worked late and monitored employees' whereabouts, determining the best time of day to open the safe and make off with the loot.

The large-scale commercial laundry ran a profitable side business moving major amounts of money without it touching the banking system. Cash is king, her boss Andy liked to say.

Her chest grew tight. Andy would suspect her and pursue her to the ends of the earth. Money mattered more to him than people's lives. She'd heard him brag about a secret method he used to eliminate the competition. He'd defend his lifestyle and kill her to teach others a lesson.

She glanced at Phil, who was sound asleep, and made a decision. Getting the money back meant trusting Dan. They needed him. He was driving out of the way for them, and he seemed like a nice guy. If he tried anything in the motel room, she'd knock him out, using a vase or whatever was at hand.

"Fine, we'll get one hotel room, but it has to have two beds," she said, wagging a finger. "You can have one. Phil and I will share a bed."

Phil woke up, hearing his name. "Share a bed? I'm not sharing a bed with him."

"I can hear you," Dan said, "The feeling is mutual."

Jas raised her eyebrows. She looked over at Phil. What had they gotten themselves into?

Dan said, "But who's gonna pay for the hotel room? Who has the truck and the transportation, Jas?"

"You do, Dan," she said. "You've got the wheels. We'll get the room."

His phone rang. "Would you answer that, Jas? I don't like to talk while I'm driving. Statistics about distracted drivers and accidents, you know."

"Hello, Dan's phone," Jas answered.

"Where is my son? Where are you taking him?"

"We're on our way to the Oregon coast."

"Why are you going there?"

"We have a golfer in our midst."

Rolling her eyes at Phil, she realized she was getting punchy from too little sleep, too much stress and too many surprises in one night. Where was their cash? She needed to find the thieves.

"I need my son home in three days. He has to turn over the manure pile out back. And will you be coming with him? You sound like a nice girl."

"Bye, Mom," Dan said.

Jas winced. Anything but this version of fate, where she robbed a safe and ended up stuck on an isolated ranch.

She hung up. "Your mom said you need to be home tomorrow. We appreciate the ride, but you can drop us off and turn around and go home the scenic way."

Dan chuckled. "I heard her. She said three days. Gives us time to have fun and see the ocean before we go home."

Keeping his eyes on the road as he drove, Dan said, "I'd planned to take you home with me."

Jas said, "I'm sorry we can't do that. We have to follow the golf tour."

Dan pointed to a road sign indicating a junction ahead.

"That's our ticket to the Oregon coast. Hang on boys and girls, here we go."

8

————

BETS

Bets was still driving before dawn. They had a long way to go. Zerk had rigged up a tarp to cover the shattered window. It flapped in the wind and fell off on the pavement. She braked and pulled over. Zerk ran to pick up the tarp. He stuffed it in back and got in the passenger seat.

Her stomach grumbled. Bets recalled how they'd almost been caught after a robbery when they'd pulled over and waited for a Starbucks to open. They'd wanted one of those breakfast sandwiches with egg and cheese, being hungry from working all night on a heist.

Whatever they put in those sandwiches was addictive. Her mouth had watered, thinking about it. Just as they were leaving Starbuck's, they saw a cop car heading their way with flashing lights, and they'd pulled over into the bushes, hiding until the road was clear. They'd gotten away with a haul of five-hundred dollars, lifted from the manager of a Super Taco on his way to the bank night deposit.

"I can put up with the wind whistling in my ears," Bets

said, "given the pile of money we have. Nothing's going to bother me for the rest of my days."

"Glad to hear it. No more temper, huh?" He eyed her as if he didn't believe her.

"All gone. I'll be as boring as Buddha, like a meditating monk. You won't even recognize me when we get set up in Millersville."

Hours later, Bets turned into a Starbucks drive-through and ordered breakfast sandwiches and coffees. Black for him, and two sugars for her.

Zerk turned to her, raising his eyebrows. "Two sugars? Look at you, living large."

"I'm having whatever I want from now on, no diets or counting calories. But wasn't this the worst night?" She rubbed her eyes. "My eyes are stinging from whatever they used to clean the carpet in that dump. If we'd slept at a rest stop, we wouldn't have a busted window and could've slept all night."

Zerk patted the dog. "I thought we'd celebrate in a motel room, but it didn't work out that way."

"Not with the lumberjack and his dog next door. I'll feel better when I'm far away from that motel. I'm scratching, like I've got cooties."

He rubbed his arms. "I know what you mean. Maybe the laundry detergent was too harsh."

She paid for the food and drinks and merged onto I-5 North.

"When we get to that small town, we'll be safe there," she said.

"We don't know much about it."

Wind whipped through the open window, making it hard to hear him.

"We can always move, if it doesn't feel right," he said.

She said, "I'd like to put down roots. I'm tired of being on the lookout and worried about being caught."

He patted her hand. "I know. Me too. It's stressful always keeping an eye out."

Hours later, Zerk pointed to a billboard. "Five Star Liquors, lowest prices. I could use a pit stop and some bourbon."

She pulled into the parking lot and wrinkled her nose at the sight of three porta-potties lined up outside a white one-story building with a blue roof. She'd envisioned first-class accommodations on this trip, given the money they had. When they got to Millersville, everything would be different. Upscale, all the way, baby.

Zerk went into the store and carried a box out on his shoulders. He set the box in back by the missing window.

"Tequila for you, Maker's Mark for me."

She tossed him the car keys. "I might drink something different to fit our new circumstances. I'm a wealthy woman now."

She laughed. With the haul in the back of the car and their final job behind them, they'd retired. No more risks were ahead.

As Bets got in the passenger seat and set Mimi on her lap, she realized she had no idea who she wanted to be for the rest of her life. She could create any kind of persona for herself. What did rich people drink? Champagne? No, that gave her a headache. She'd upgrade to the more expensive tequilas, the reposados, to reflect her new status.

She tilted her head. What had she always wanted but been missing? Growing up in a rural area and homeschooled by an overbearing mother, she'd wanted to escape their ramshackle home. When she turned sixteen and set off for the city, she'd earned her way as a live-in maid and groundskeeper until she met Zerk and joined him in a life of crime. They weren't the best burglars, but they'd tried hard to excel at their craft.

They drove all day, switching drivers at rest stops. Bets' stomach growled, and he announced it was dinner time. But she had more important things to do than eat. She wanted to get to their destination and find a place to hide their money.

She turned off the freeway and followed the signs to Millersville. The dog woke up on Zerk's lap and barked. Bets tapped her fingers on the steering wheel.

"Not yet, Mimi," she said, "another hour or so yet. Then we'll be in your new hometown."

"What'll we do with our time?" Zerk said. "I might get bored if I don't have anything to do all day."

"Make birdhouses, or buy a set of drums. It's a rich person's problem, worrying about finding meaning and purpose in life. Don't you think?"

"I guess. I've never had time off or a vacation before now," he said, looking confused. "I always worked in a warehouse and on my time off, robbed places. I'm uncomfortable about having nothing to do. I think it's perfectly understandable."

She patted his hand. "You're right, it is. Maybe you can join a men's group or a book club or play billiards, but for God's sake, don't tell anyone who we are or where we're from. Remember our cover story?"

He put a warm hand on her shoulder and squeezed. "Love you, B. We'll say we're tired of working on our ranch, and we're looking for a place to settle down and take early retirement." He smiled. "I can be convincing."

She chuckled. "You can be, like the day you proposed.

You jumped out of a tree, nearly killed me with fright, and flew a paper airplane with a proposal on it. Very clever."

He grinned as they headed west toward a sunset of purples, pinks, reds and blues. "Clever is how we ended up with the stash in our car, settling us up for years. You noticed the car idling outside the laundry at night with the trunk open."

She nodded. "They didn't look back once to see if they had a tail."

"We need to establish new identities."

"I agree. We'll stay under the radar." She shook a finger at him as a reminder to keep his big mouth shut. "We'll blend in. No one will notice us. Is that right?"

The dog barked.

9

———

JAS

As dawn broke, Dan pulled off to the side of the road. Jas climbed out of the tow truck and groaned. Her joints ached, and her neck had a kink. It hurt to look to her right.

Dan sniffed the pine-scented air and opened his arms. "We're in Oregon."

"Watch out for poison oak," Phil said.

She waded into the bushes and squatted to do her business. Going back to the truck where Phil and Dan waited, her feet were covered with pine needles. Wearing sandals for a getaway operation was one of her many mistakes.

She said to Phil, "Your turn to sit in the middle."

He held up his hands. "I won't mess with a woman who hasn't enough sleep."

He scooted into the truck and patted the seat beside him.

Jas hopped in. He was right. She hated when anything screwed with her plans.

Last week, she'd invited friends to go dancing. They'd met at Spritzer's for drinks. When the other three, including

Phil, wanted see a movie instead of dance, the sudden change left her feeling out of control. She'd gone to see *Spider Man Ten* with them, but she wasn't good company, sitting with her arms crossed.

Like the numbers on balance sheets at work, she liked life to be organized, which reminded her of her boss. She'd helped Andy keep a separate set of books with his real transactions. She cringed. He'd suspect her when she didn't show up at work after his business was robbed.

"Jas, you mentioned a task you must accomplish," Dan said as he drove. "What is it?"

Phil crossed his arms in the middle seat.

Jas leaned against the passenger door.

"I'll understand if you didn't trust me," Dan said. "We only just met."

Jas and Phil exchanged a look. She didn't want to involve another person, or split the money with Dan, or take the risk of him reporting the robbery to the police.

"After I finish the golf match, we'll talk," Phil said, winking at her.

She rolled the window down a few inches. The smell of salt air wafted through the cab. She pointed to a sign and a series of elegant lodge-like buildings.

"There's Ocean Dunes Golf Resort."

Dan patted Phil's knee.

"Can't wait to see you golf, buddy. You're a star. I'm honored to be driving you here."

When he stopped in the parking lot, Jas said, "I'll see about getting us a room. You guys wait here."

Dan hopped out. "We're friends. We're doing everything together from now on."

Jas shot Phil a raised eyebrow, and the three of them marched into the hotel lobby.

"We'd like three rooms, please, one for each of us," she said at the counter.

Dan started to object, but the hotel clerk, who was dressed in a white shirt, black tie and blazer said, "I'm sorry, we have only one unit left. The Dune Suite with four bedrooms."

Dan smiled. "My ma could join us."

Jas cringed. It was all happening too fast. She needed to sleep for ten hours and eat a decent meal, then she'd be fine. "And the cost?"

"Five hundred and forty dollars a night," the clerk said, "plus tax."

"That's steep," Dan said. "Are you sure you don't have anything smaller? With a king-size bed we could share?"

The man, in his thirties, wrinkled his nose and glanced at the parking lot.

"We don't, I'm sorry to say. We have a golf tournament starting today."

Jas said, "Dan, can your mother pay, using the money from selling Phil's car?"

Dan turned to the clerk.

"Will you hold the room for us? I need to make a quick call."

He went over to the window overlooking the parking lot and pulled out his phone.

"Mom, did you sell their car? We're at the Ocean Dunes Golf Resort in Oregon, and we'd like to use some of that money to pay for a room." He listened and looked at Jas and Phil. "It wasn't where I said it'd be? Why not?" He nodded. "I'll tell them."

Dan hung up and came over to Jas and Phil.

"You're not going to believe this, but your car was gone by the time my mother got there. She thinks someone stole it. We'll have to find another way to pay for the room."

Jas rested a hand on Phil's shoulder. "I'm sorry I dragged you into this. You've lost your car and your job. It's all my fault."

Phil blinked. "I'll get over it. It's just a car."

Dan patted Phil's back. "Sorry. That's rough. Good thing you're going with me."

Jas pulled out her credit card. "I'll pay for the room. We need to sleep, and Phil here," she nudged him, "has a tournament to compete in."

Phil was dazed. He stared at the tiled floor.

The clerk took her card and ran it through the system.

"One night or two?"

"One," Jas said, at the same time Dan said, "Two."

"One," Jas repeated, giving Dan a hard look. There was no way she'd spend more than one night in the same suite as a stranger. She'd lock her door and put a chair up against it. Tomorrow, she'd be out of here with Phil, following the two thieves.

The clerk handed her an invoice to sign. "Sir, are you Phil Mickelson by chance? We've been expecting you for the competition. I heard her say your name and that you'd be competing?"

Phil broke into a coughing fit. He turned away.

"Sure, he is," Dan said. "I gave him a ride here in my truck."

The clerk stared at the tow truck, taking up two spaces.

"Is that your truck out there? Dew Drop Towing?"

"That's my rig," Dan said.

"We'll have to ask you to move it to the outer parking lot, sir, so it won't get damaged. The parking spots are too small near the office for a vehicle as grand as that."

Dan smiled.

Phil shuffled toward the exit.

Jas sighed. The first thing she needed to do after getting to their room was use Dan's phone and call her dad. She'd break his heart with the news she didn't have the money to pay for his medical care.

10

BETS

In the Two Rivers Resort office, a man in his forties wearing wire-rimmed glasses handed Bets a key to Cabin Eight. She thanked him and went outside. While Zerk walked the dog down on a dirt lane, a teenage boy reached into their car.

Bets yelped and ran over.

A pale, skinny teenager pulled a tequila bottle through the broken back window.

"Scat," Bets said to the youth. "Go on, get out of here."

"You've got plenty. I just want one." He glanced over his shoulder at the office.

Zerk strode to the car. Mimi yipped as he said, "If you're gonna steal, pick another place. This is too obvious, and we're the wrong people to tangle with."

The office door opened. "Jeremy? Time for dinner. Your mother's calling."

The boy blushed. "That's my dad. He runs the place. Bye."

Bets pointed to a log cabin in a grove of evergreen trees. "We're over there, in Cabin Eight."

They unloaded the car as fast as they could, putting trash bags of money in a corner of the one-room cabin. She covered the bags with a blanket from the back of the car and added their suitcases on top. As a savvy thief, she made it a practice to carry to-go bags with a change of clothes and toiletries in the car, in case they needed to disappear at a moment's notice.

She opened his suitcase and got out his gold nail clippers, a gift she'd given him after they robbed a food bank last year. He liked to trim his toenails each night and didn't sleep well unless he tended to that first. Last night had been an exception, in the motel room. It was the first and last for many things, like the dueling barking dogs and broken car window.

"Tomorrow," Zerk said, "we'll fix the car window."

"Maybe go to the bank and put part of it in a big safe deposit box?"

Zerk gave her a sidelong glance.

"How would we carry that much cash into a bank? It would fill several garbage cans. Here's what I'm thinking. I know it's fast, but tomorrow we'll check out the town and decide no or yes. Then we'll build that house you've been wanting so much as quick as we can. Paying cash will motivate a builder to get it done, especially if we offer a cash bonus to finish early."

She threw her arms around him.

"That's what I've been wanting. We'll buy a plot of land and hire a builder and get started right away."

"If we like the area," he said. "We're not settling for anywhere but paradise."

She clapped her hands, and Mimi barked.

"Only paradise for us from now on. We did those kids a

favor by lifting their loot. They wouldn't have known what to do with it."

He grinned. "Leave it to the professionals."

She laughed. "Because we know what we're doing."

11

JAS

Jas went into the Dune Suite and sucked in a breath, taking in the stunning views of the forest and dunes. But this wasn't a time to appreciate beauty. They needed to find the thieves and get their money back. Her dad was depending on her.

Phil came up beside her while Dan strode ahead, looking around.

He said in a low voice, "I need twenty minutes on my laptop with Wi-Fi to get an idea of where the robbers are. I'll go out and pretend to golf and get rid of Dan. I'll come back to the room, and we'll get started tracking them."

She nodded. "Sounds like a plan, using your super sleuth computer skills. That's why I picked you to help. And I trust you."

Phil smiled.

Dan came back, grinning.

"I love this place. Free coffee, a huge television with cable and a mini-frig filled with booze. They even have little bags of popcorn and chocolate bars."

"Quite the place," Phil said. "I'm going golfing. Dan, want to come?"

"Sure thing."

"I'm going to the gift shop," Jas said, "to get new clothes. These are filthy." She couldn't wait to change her shirt and get out of her grubby sandals.

Dan held up his keycard. "Do we all have our keys in case we get separated?"

Phil and Jas held theirs up.

"Let's go golfing, Phil. I'll be your extra caddy."

They left the suite, and Jas hurried to the gift shop. She wanted to be quick and get back to the room before Dan got back to check her bank balances to be sure the thieves hadn't hacked into her accounts. She also wanted to check her emails and see if her boss had sent anything. Did he know yet that the safe was empty? She'd taken the fake set of books in her bag as insurance, but that was going to tick off her boss.

"Can I help you?" a sales clerk asked, looking Jas up and down. She was about fifty and tan, her face lined from spending time in the sun.

"I need a new outfit," Jas said, "and I'm in a hurry. Would you please pick out a new shirt and pants and shoes, too, and ring them up? I'm a size nine shoe."

"Right this way," the clerk said. "My name is Francis, and I'm happy to help you."

Jas looked out the window and saw Phil exit the building with Dan. She didn't know how long it would take for Phil to make an excuse, get away from Dan and go back to the room. They'd eaten breakfast from a Burger King drive-through on the way here, so saying he was hungry and going toward the dining room probably wasn't an option.

"Here's what we have in your size." Francis held up a

pink polo short emblazoned with an Ocean Dunes Golf Resort logo in white, a purple golf skort, white socks and gray spike-less golf shoes.

Jas covered her mouth, trying not to giggle.

"Do you have anything other than purple and something other than a skort? I'm more of a shorts or pants type person."

"Sorry," Francis said, but she didn't look sorry at all, "Supply chain problems and shipment delays. We have very little left, so you're lucky to get these."

Outside, Phil was running toward the resort.

Jas handed over her credit card.

"Ring them up, please. I've got to go back to my room right now."

Francis hummed while she worked. The pace was too slow for Jas. She signed for the credit card charge, grabbed the items and rushed back to the suite.

A minute after she got inside and tossed the new clothes and shoes on the floor, Phil flung himself through the door and double-locked it with a security chain.

"Let's get to work," he said. "I'm not sure how much time we have until he finds us."

Phil opened his laptop and, using his computer skills, tracked their cell phones and internet searches done on their phones. "Okay, the phones are at a place called Two Rivers Resort in a town called Millersville, Washington. A few hours north of Seattle."

"Excellent," Jas said, pacing the room. "I love that we know that. Anything else?"

"They looked up Millersville and a Super 9 budget motel."

"A Super 9?" Jas half-smiled. "We're here, and they

stayed at a place like that? We're doing better than them at this point."

"Except we need to get to Millersville, and we don't have a car."

"Good point." She pulled out her laptop. "I'll check my bank accounts and make sure they didn't hack in."

A keycard clicked.

The door opened but got caught on the security chain.

"Hey, let me in," Dan said.

Jas and Phil looked at each and shut their laptops, putting them away.

"Guys?" Dan said.

"Coming," Phil said, undoing the chain.

"Don't lock me out," Dan said, coming in the room. "We're family, after what we've been through, driving all night. We're like cousins. Why did you run off?"

Jas opened a sliding door and stepped out onto a balcony, looking over the forest and dunes. A blue sky with streaks of white clouds topped off the perfect picture. This would be paradise if those thieves hadn't come along and taken what was theirs, and if Dan hadn't insisted on sticking with them, to the point of staying in the same hotel suite.

Her throat was tight with tears. Her father needed that money. The experimental medical care was his last hope of extending his life.

Phil joined her on the balcony. "Dan's ordering room service."

She said in a hushed voice, "I've got to tell my dad."

"What about your dad?" Dan said, coming onto the balcony.

The planks shook as he walked on them.

Jas wiped her eyes. "My dad's sick. He has a rare, deadly lung disease, and his insurance won't pay for a treatment that might help him. I promised to pay for it. He never smoked. It isn't right, him being sick like this."

"It sucks," Phil said in a choked voice.

"Oh man," Dan said, looking up at the sky, "It sounds tough. With him being sick, I don't know what I'd do if I were you."

She watched as Dan brushed away a tear. The big lug was tender-hearted. Maybe he would help them find the money. An idea occurred to her, and she said, "I need to talk with Phil for a moment. Excuse us, please."

They stepped to the edge of the balcony, about four feet from Dan, who sat down on a lounge chair that creaked.

Shoulder to shoulder, facing beach grass that swayed in a steady breeze, she said in a low voice, "I think we should tell him what happened."

Phil's eyebrows shot up. "No, I don't think so. We don't even know him."

"We'll tell him part of the truth," she whispered to Phil. "If he knows about the missing money, he might help us get it back. Or drive us to Millersville. He seems nice enough."

"I'm right over here, you know," Dan said from his lounge chair. "Don't whisper about me. It hurts my feelings to be left out."

Phil touched her hand. "I hope you're sure about this, because it could go very wrong. I don't want to end up in jail."

She nodded to him. "Believe me, I don't want that either. I'll do whatever it takes to avoid jail."

Turning to Dan, she said, "Here's the story. We had the money to pay for my father's medical care, but two thieves took it last night."

Dan sat up. "Who were they? What happened?"

"Two people pulled us over and acted like police officers," she said, rushing the words and hoping she'd made the right choice to share this information. "They took our money, handcuffed us and took our phones. We need to get that money back."

She waved her arms for emphasis.

Phil crossed his arms and looked like he wished she hadn't told Dan the truth.

"That's why you were on the side of the road," Dan said. "They left you there?"

"They did, and I need to find them, get my money back and help my dad. Will you help us?"

Dan scratched his chin. "That's what you meant in the truck, when you said you had a task you must accomplish. You're out to recover a load of money some crooks took from you." He cocked his head. "But Phil, you're a famous golfer. Can't you give her the money for her father?"

Phil said, "I'm not that Phil. I work with computers. I was faking it."

"Is that why you ran away from me on the golf course and went in the room, locking me out? You didn't trust me with the truth?"

Jas nodded, wondering if she'd made a huge mistake with her rash decision just now. This man could be a criminal for all she knew. But what were their choices?

"We wanted to research where the robbers went, and we didn't want you knowing what we were up to. It's a risk, bringing more people in."

She picked at her chapped lips. Dan might turn them into the authorities now that he knew the real story. Or use it for leverage to extract hush money, which she didn't have.

Phil arched his eyebrows and gazed at her with what might've been affection.

She folded her arms and waited for what the tow truck

driver would say. Would he walk out? Or double-cross them?

"I'd like to help," Dan said. "I've saved some money you could have. Would twenty-thousand dollars be enough?"

Jas let out a loud whoosh of breath.

"Wow, that's generous of you. It'd be a start. But I need two-hundred-thousand dollars for my dad. We can't take your money. It wouldn't be right."

He shrugged. "I don't need it. But where are these people? Did you find out?"

"They're up in Washington State, north of Seattle a few hours." Her voice was shaking from the tension. Would he offer to take them north? "In a town called Millersville."

"I'd be glad to drive you there in my truck. I'll have to call my mom first, though, to let her know where I'm going. We'll have an adventure together." Dan smiled.

"We will, won't we?" Phil said, with a half-smile.

The room phone rang.

Jas went inside and picked it up.

"Ms. Bucker, I'm sorry to inform you, but we just received notice of a fraud alert on your credit card. The card has been compromised. We won't deliver your room service order. And you need to vacate the suite immediately."

Jas hung up and went out on the deck.

The two men were leaning on the railing, side by side, and talking in low voices.

"The hotel is kicking us out. My credit card must've been hacked by the thieves."

"What about my food?" Dan said. "I ordered a Reuben sandwich with fries. And chicken Caesar salads for you guys. I had to guess at what you'd like."

"Thanks, Dan," Jas said. "I would've liked that with a diet Dr. Pepper."

Dan smacked his forehead.

"I didn't see that coming. I would've pegged you as a diet Coke type person."

"Hello?" Phil said, looking from Jas to Dan. "Why are we talking about diet drinks? We've got to get out of here."

Jas held up an index finger. "I'm not going until I take a shower and change my clothes. Don't let anyone in until I finish doing that."

Jas locked the bathroom door and stood in the hot shower. She wasn't sure of herself anymore. All her plans had scattered in the wind. What would she tell her father?

She dried off with a white bath towel and dressed in the new pink polo shirt, the hideous purple skort, white socks and gray sneakers. Quite the outfit for the trip north. Small red blisters itched on her bum and her feet. Great, poison oak, just what she needed now.

She stepped into the living room, where Phil and Dan were waiting, freshly showered with wet hair. She grabbed her messenger bag and wrapped a clean white fluffy big bath towel around her neck like she'd just been at the beach. Might as well take a souvenir of the place where they didn't get to stay. It might come in handy.

She said, "Let's head to Millersville, find the thieves and take the money back."

12

BETS

Early the next morning, Bets and Zerk counted the cash on the round kitchen table at Cabin Eight. Stacks of five, ten, twenty and fifty-dollar bills piled high. They moved some onto the floor to complete the process.

"Quite the haul," Bets said, opening her arms wide. "We got lucky, baby."

Zerk grinned. "Five-hundred thou lucky."

They pushed the money into black plastic trash bags and covered them with a bedspread, setting their suitcases on top.

Locking the cabin door, they hurried to the car.

The teenage boy leaned against a nearby tree, breaking a twig into tiny pieces.

"Hey, kid," Bets said, holding up a ten-dollar bill. "You want a job? Watch the cabin for us until we get back. Make sure no one breaks in."

Zerk said to her in a low voice, "Good thinking."

The boy came over and took the money. "Sure, I'll do that."

"We appreciate the help," Zerk said.

Bets climbed in the passenger seat and put Mimi the dog on her lap.

Zerk chuckled as he drove toward town.

"I'm glad we put that kid to work. At that age, I was pushing a broom at the Arctic Circle drive-in, sweeping the parking lot." He sighed. "I'd like one of their burgers and shakes right now."

She frowned. "If he gets nosy and breaks in, he'll find the cash. We'll have to kill him, which is something we haven't done before. I don't want to do that."

"We'll stick to our area of expertise. We're ethical robbers. We're not killers."

She nodded. "I totally agree with you. And we've got him on our side now. If we decide to live here, we'll need to find a house to rent, somewhere no one will find us."

"Let's take a look around, see what we think."

An older two-story home had a sign in front advertising Gigi's Café.

"Isn't that cute?" she said. "We could have breakfast there."

"No outdoor seating. I'd rather eat outside with Mimi."

She patted the dog. "You're right. We'll find another place."

He pulled over at Dad's Diner, and they ate outside with Mimi at a picnic table.

Bets ate a bite of beef brisket. "Oh, this is so good."

Mimi sat and begged.

Bets said, "Just this once, I'll give her a taste, to celebrate our success."

"That's what you always say."

Zerk forked a chunk of crisp roast potato with creamy

horseradish sauce into his mouth and groaned. "Glad we came here."

A gray-haired man at the next table said, "Cute dog. Do you mind if I pet her?"

He reminded Bets of the lumberjack, tall and wide-shouldered with a mustache.

"She bites, so that's not a good idea. Do you live around here?"

The man nodded. "All my life."

"Do you like it?"

"Well, sure, who wouldn't? Friendly people, a beautiful place, not too far from Seattle, if you want to drive through traffic. Far enough away to feel like the country but with everything you'd want."

Zerk wiped his mouth. "Quite the endorsement."

"Where're you folks from?"

Bets shot Zerk a cautionary look. He was the blabbermouth of the two of them.

"We're nomads these days, driving around, getting a feel for this wonderful country of ours. Deciding where to settle down."

The man nodded and thrust out his hand. "Harold Biggins, nice to meet you."

Bets said, "I'm Jas, and this is Phil."

After breakfast, they stopped at a hardware store and bought a lock, a roll of duct tape, plastic to cover the missing car window, and a battery-powered outdoor security camera.

With her favorite station on, Talking Lips Radio, Bets drove while they explored different neighborhoods. Coming to an area overlooking the bay, Bets rolled down the windows and took a deep breath.

"Salt air smells good, doesn't it?" she said, smiling at Zerk.

He inhaled and released a sigh. "No more desert dwelling for us. We've earned a new life. Our hard work paid off."

A tugboat pulling a barge went past, plying the blue water.

"We've had our bumps in the road," she said, "but learned from them. We know what we're doing. It's a shame we're retiring."

"But it's time. I'm ready to quit a life of crime, aren't you?"

She nodded. "I am, but I worry that the haul we've got isn't enough to tide us over forever. If we build a place, we'll have to watch our spending. And maybe get real jobs."

He cocked his head. "Maybe we'll find something different. We're good with people, aren't we?"

"Honey," she said, patting his arm. "We're the best."

She turned down a street and stopped a block from the water at a vacant lot with a sign. "For Sale by Skilled Built Houses. Inquire about our buy & build plan."

Zerk grinned. "Feels like home already. Do you like the lot? Shall I call?"

"Hold on, I want to look around."

She got out, and they walked the land.

"Look at this," she said, holding his hand. "A large lot. A huge rock between us and the neighbors. We'll have privacy in spades. That's a yes from me."

LATER THAT MORNING, they met with the builder at the lot. Bets didn't mention it to Zerk, but she was harboring doubts because the process was too easy. She was superstitious, and something felt off. Since they'd stolen the money from the young couple, everything had gone remarkably well. For her, that boded ill. It could fall apart at any minute.

It gave her a headache to think of all the ways they could blow their windfall by saying the wrong remark to an upstanding citizen. Just like that, with a snap of his or her fingers, it could evaporate. She'd do anything she could to avoid attracting attention or being arrested.

"We had a project fall through," the contractor said. "So, I could get started pretty soon. What kind of design do you have in mind? Two-story? One-level living? Modern or traditional? I have designs I can show you."

Bets signaled to Zerk that she'd take over. After all, this was her dream home. He could chip in, but she wanted to have the bigger say.

"We'd like it to be built into the hill and primarily made out of concrete. It would be one-level."

Bill, the contractor, furrowed his brow. "We could do that. Building into the hill won't give you many windows though."

She said, "That's fine."

"Any other ideas?"

She said, "We want one door to the outside. A second one will lead to the attached garage, but we want only one direct way into the house. We're big on security."

Bill scratched his chin. "One front door and no back or side doors, is that right? Built into the hill, so the rear windows are level with the grass?"

"Yes, and we'd like a back room with no windows, just a skylight, and a walk-in closet and ensuite bathroom, sort of like a panic room."

The contractor looked at Zerk. "Is this what you want

too? I just like to make sure couples are on the same page before we start."

Zerk said, "We're in agreement. And we'd like a solid core steel door on the panic room. Same for the front door, for extra security."

Bill said, "You realize this will be a dark house inside, with little natural light?"

"You can put in skylights," Bets said. "That should help. We'd like to get started right away." She looked at Zerk, who smiled and nodded.

"What you've described is an unusual house, but if you're sure that's what you want, we can build it. Now for the matter of payment. Will you be getting a bank loan?"

Bets shook her head. "No, we'll avoid that."

Zerk said, "We can skip dealing with the banks."

Bill nodded. "I like that. Less hassle and paperwork, with fewer people involved."

"How long are we looking at for construction?" Zerk said.

"Around nine to ten months," Bill said. "I've got to get the permits and all."

"Could you accelerate the timing, if you had a financial incentive?" Bets folded her arms and hoped the man would say yes.

"Sure, we could build it faster if I put more crew on it."

Bets nodded to Zerk, who pulled out a non-disclosure agreement they'd found on the internet and printed at the library before meeting with the contractor.

"Before we go ahead," Zerk said, "we'd like you to sign a non-disclosure agreement saying you won't discuss our names, our home or how we paid for it with anyone."

Bill took the form and read it over. "I've worked with

famous people before, so I'll sign it. There won't be a problem. Everyone deserves privacy."

Bets said, "We'll pay you a bonus if you finish early."

"Let me see how quick we can do this for you," Bill said. "Where are you staying?"

"Two Rivers Resort for now," Zerk said. "We're looking for a place to rent until the house is finished."

"I have a place you could rent, if you're concerned about privacy and security. I built it for my mother."

Bets looked at Zerk and raised her shoulders in a why-not gesture, in the way couples who've been together for years know each other's meaning.

"Sure," Zerk said, "let's take a look."

13

JAS

Jas drove the tow truck, heading east on a winding two-lane road cut through rock and evergreen trees. She didn't mind working the pedals of the big rig and coasting on the curves because her father taught her to drive his cement truck when she was eighteen.

Coming out of the forest, she followed signs to I-5 North and merged onto the freeway. The group was quiet, as if mulling over all they had to do. The odds were against their finding the robbers and recovering the money, but she had to follow through for her father's sake.

"Thanks for doing this, guys. I really appreciate it. I couldn't do it without you."

"Of course," Phil said. "Your dad needs you. We want to help."

"That's what family is all about," Dan said. "You can't save your dad's life if you don't get the money back. I'd do the same for my mother if I was in your situation."

Phil stretched his long legs, sitting next to her.

"I'm nervous about what we'll do," Phil said, "if and

when we find the robbers. They knew what they were doing and had guns. I'm just a computer nerd."

Dan looked at Jas and Phil with wide eyes.

"Are these people dangerous? Are we risking our lives? I didn't think about that before I signed up. My mother wouldn't be pleased."

Jas took a moment to swallow. Her throat was dry. She could use a diet Dr. Pepper right about now.

"Dan, if you want out, that's fine." Phil elbowed her, but she continued. "Those two, who I believe are called Bets and Zerk, are dangerous. She held a gun on us."

"What?" Dan said. "And you didn't mention this before because?"

She said, "I'm sorry. I need this the money so much, and we didn't have any idea you'd be coming with us. It's not like we're used to doing this sort of thing. I've never stolen more than a popsicle at the corner grocery store before."

"Pack of gum for me," Phil said. "When I was seven and didn't know better."

"I guess I knew it was dangerous, given it involved money, but golly, this is a surprise," Dan said. "The gun is a game changer."

Going up a hill, Jas slowed behind a semi-truck and changed lanes.

"You don't have to go with us. I don't want you to get hurt. You don't even know my dad."

Dan said, "If I were sick, I'd sure as heck want someone doing this for me. I'd want to enjoy the world around me for as long as I could." He nodded. "You know what? We'll do this as a team, no matter what. I'm in."

Jas blew out a breath. "That's a relief. We need you."

"Welcome aboard," Phil said, patting Dan's coveralled knee.

"It's my truck, buddy, so welcome aboard to you too." He laughed.

He held up two fingers in a victory sign.

As they chuckled, Jas pointed to a road sign.

"Rest Stop ahead. Anyone need to use the facilities?"

Phil said, "I could use a break."

Turning on the blinker and slowing down, she squirmed and said, "Let's switch drivers. This poison oak rash is killing me."

Right now, she had bigger worries on her mind, like what would happen when they got to Millersville. Would anyone die? Was she wrong for dragging Phil and Dan into her mess and risking their lives?

"I'll drive next," Dan said. "Although Jasmine, you're looking pretty good behind the wheel. It looks like you know what you're doing."

In the middle seat, Phil frowned.

Jas wondered if he was jealous? If so, he'd have to get over it. They needed to find the robbers, and Dan was offering his services.

Jas wondered if Dan's generosity came with a price. What was in it for Dan, besides going on an adventure and seeking justice? While pretending to be an innocent truck driver, he might be after the money. His aw-shucks facade might be an act.

She shook her head. Her father's health problems and his ticking clock with months left to live were making her cynical. Dan was authentic. She was sure of it.

She drove toward the parking area for trucks at the rest stop.

"I wanted to be a truck driver, but my dad talked me into going into accounting."

"Good choice," Dan said. "That or computers are steady

work. And you don't have to work outside like I do in all kinds of weather."

"What you do is hard work," Phil said. "Truck drivers are the unsung heroes of the highways."

Jas nodded.

"Few appreciate it," Dan said, "so thank you for your kind words. It's a calling."

Jas parked and put on the emergency brake.

"Dan, can I use your phone? I'd like to call my dad and the bank."

He handed it to her. "If my mother calls, don't tell her where we are or she might follow us. She hates to be left out."

She dialed her father.

When he picked up, she said, "Dad? It's Jasmine."

Her father broke into a coughing fit.

"I'm sorry," she said in a shaky voice. "But I can't pay for the place in Mexico. I wish I could, and I know I promised you, but something came up."

"It's okay, honey. I wish I could take out a loan, but in my condition, no one would give me the money. Can you ask that boss of yours to give you an advance?"

Jas sighed. Her boss wouldn't help someone else, especially not for that amount of money. Five dollars maybe, but not for two-hundred-thousand bucks. Her dad wasn't being realistic, but then again, he was facing down a death sentence.

Doctors said his habit of inhaling fumes from microwave popcorn bags over the years may have caused his rare deadly lung disease. He liked the aroma, so he'd stick his nose in a just-opened hot bag and breathe in deeply from two or more bags a day.

She gripped the phone tight. "I lost my job, so I can't ask my boss or get a loan."

"But you were so good at it." He coughed. "Did he fire you? I'll go talk to that turd of a boss of yours."

"Please don't do that." She wiped her sweating hands on her skort. "Don't go anywhere near the company. It wouldn't be safe now. If the police come see you, say you don't know where I am. Same with my boss."

"Where are you?"

"I can't tell you. I don't want you getting into trouble. Pretend we never talked."

"Whose phone are you calling from?" he said. "I don't recognize the number. I hope you didn't do anything stupid, trying to get the money. What did you do?"

Her throat clogged with tears. "Dad, I've got to go. Stay safe, and I'll call you as soon as I can. I love you."

She hung up and burst out crying.

"Everything alright?" Phil said, coming up beside her.

She rested her forehead on his shoulder and leaned into him for a reassuring hug. They were good friends who enjoyed each other's company. She'd handle this, somehow, with her heart breaking and with little time left with her father.

"I told my dad I didn't have the money. He's going to die, but I can't help him."

She sniffled. Before she broke down weeping, she thrust the phone at him.

"Give this to Dan? I'll be right back."

She ran into the women's restroom and splashed water on her face.

As she came out, she overheard Dan saying into the phone, "Mom, calm down. Everything's going to be fine. I'm just taking a longer vacation than we anticipated. Work will be there when I get home."

Jas slowed her pace to better eavesdrop.

Dan listened and then said, "We're going to Washington state. I've never been there. No, the people in my truck aren't taking advantage of me. I'm sure of that. Stop worrying about me. They're like family."

Jas heard Dan's mother yelling and hoped it wouldn't change his mind. A part of her wanted to hurt the thieves for what they'd taken, maybe even kill them. But she and Phil weren't killers. She'd only taken the money because of her father. And to get away and make a fresh start, somewhere far from places that would remind her of her dad. The farther away, the better, tucked away on a sandy beach where the police and her boss couldn't track them.

Dan nodded to Jas. "Got to go. No, don't do that. Don't follow me to Millersville. I'm fine with my friends. Stop worrying, I'm a grown man."

Jas hopped in the truck and took the middle seat. She wiggled to pull down the skort and resisted the urge to scratch her itching ankles and feet.

A few miles down the road, she used Dan's phone to talk with her credit card company's fraud division. The bank promised to send a new card to her current address, but she said to hold off. She was in the process of moving. She couldn't go back to her apartment again. She'd burned her past with the brazen caper.

In hindsight, she might be in the running for the worst thief of all time. She'd forgotten to pack her things, being so occupied with her father's health concerns, and now she couldn't return. Somehow, she'd imagined she could go back to her place and pack and then leave Vegas for good. Not smart. A good burglar wouldn't have done that.

"The bastards took my driver's license," she said, "and I want to make sure they didn't get into my bank account. I need to check on my laptop using Wi-Fi. Okay if we stop at a Starbucks?"

Phil rubbed his stomach. "I like their sandwiches."

Jas sighed. Her dad had been addicted to microwave popcorn. If only they'd had chocolate pudding or banana cream pies instead, he wouldn't have a rare disease, and she wouldn't be driving with a stranger to a town up north. She wouldn't be a thief if not for those bags of popcorn. That's what led to their downfall. A few kernels of popcorn ruined her family.

Well, except for her mom, who passed away in a car wreck five years ago. For some reason her mom hadn't fastened her seat belt that morning and had a head on crash driving to work at the ice cream factory. Vanilla chocolate chip had been Mom's favorite, and Jas couldn't have ice cream to this day without bursting into tears. Now the smell of popcorn made her gag.

"You and me both, buddy," Dan said to Phil. "Wish I'd had that Reuben sandwich. It would've been my first food at a resort."

"Me too," Phil said. "At least you bought new clothes before we got kicked out."

She snorted. "I like the shoes but not the stupid skort."

She pulled the hem down. It was riding up again, and her skin itched. She sat on her hands so she wouldn't scratch.

Dan said, "What is a skort?"

"It's a combination of skirt and shorts. Some women golfers wear them, I guess."

"You have nice legs," Phil said with a smile.

Dan glanced over. "True enough."

When Dan's phone rang, Jas picked it up and answered it.

"Hello, this is Dan's phone."

"Jas, is that you? It's Dad."

Her heart thumped. Why would he call when they'd just spoken? What something wrong besides the missing money?

"Dad, it's me."

"I called your regular number, and a strange woman answered. She wasn't very nice."

She frowned. Her father's voice was wobbly and constricted, like it got when he was upset and trying to cover it up. "What's wrong? I can hear it in your voice."

"Your boss showed up and tossed the place. Everything's a mess. He was looking for something and when he didn't find it, he threw a fit. Did you take something of his?"

She waited a beat, not wanting to lie to her father, while she figured out what to say.

"Lock your doors and windows," she said, "and don't let anyone in. I'll be back in a few days. There's something I need to do first."

"But," he said.

The phone beeped. Battery low.

"Sorry, Dad, I've got to go. Love you. See you in a few days. Eat healthy, okay?"

Jas hung up and wiped her leaking eyes.

"Your boss went to your dad's place?" Phil said, leaning into her.

"Yeah," Jas patted her messenger bag that contained the commercial laundry's secret second set of accounting books. "He was angry and looking for something. He trashed the place. I hope he doesn't hurt my dad."

Phil said, "This is turning out to be a bigger deal than I thought."

She nodded. It certainly was. She'd promised to take her dad to a residential medical clinic in Mexico. Vitamin-infused drinks, healthy food and injections to boost his immune system along with meditation and visualization exercises sounded simple at the outset, but now everything was complicated.

"What was your boss looking for?" Dan said. "And why was he so mad?"

Jas said, "Well, Dan, the truth is this. I stole the money from my boss. He made most of it off the books for some bad people, and I took it to help my father."

"This story keeps changing and not for the better." Dan said. "Now tell me, is there anything else I should know?"

"No," Jas said, "that's the whole story."

Dan shrugged. "I've come this far. I might as well see it through. At least we're taking a ride and seeing the country. Would you plug in my phone? My mom might call, and I don't want her to worry."

Connecting his phone to the charger, Jas wished it was as simple as a recharge to heal her dying father. There was a slim hope treatment would help him. But they had to try. She had to retrieve the cash and get back to her dad before it was too late.

14

BETS

Approaching a three-bedroom house facing the water, Bets nodded. The home was far enough from neighbors they wouldn't be likely to drop by or get too friendly. They couldn't risk exposing their true identities with a slip of the tongue, or someone seeing the money.

Bill, the contractor, unlocked the door. "After you."

Bets looked down at Mimi, who was on a red leash. "You're okay with dogs?"

He gave her a glance. "Sure, what damage could a little dog like that do?"

Bets stepped inside and went to the living room, where windows faced the water.

"Sometimes whales swim by," Bill said, when he and Zerk stopped to take in the view. "You'll see eagles, and otters, maybe porpoises."

"All this nature is great, because we like to keep to ourselves," Bets said, looking to Zerk for confirmation. "Don't we, dear?"

"That's right," Zerk said. "Does it come furnished by chance?"

In the living room was a brown leather couch and a matching loveseat. A television was mounted on the wall. Two barstools were at a breakfast bar.

The kitchen looked like something out of a magazine, with a white quartz countertop, a subway tile backsplash, and stainless-steel appliances. It was everything Bets dreamed of but knew she'd never have. Until now.

"I can rent it furnished. My mother moved into Chandlery Square, where all her friends are. She's got a studio apartment and couldn't take all her furniture."

Bets raised her eyebrows. How surprising for his mom to move from this breathtaking view of the water. Across the way was a forested island. She wondered what life was like over there. It was better to hide in plain sight, among other people in a town this size. Blending in was best. That way, no one from their past would find them.

"My mom doesn't mind living in a retirement home," Bill said. "She plays cards and has friends. She doesn't have to cook. I noticed you looking across the way." He pointed. "That's Cedar Island. I've built some houses over there. Great setting, but you have to depend on the ferry to get to the grocery store or hospital. Or schools, if you have kids."

"We don't have kids," Zerk said, giving Bets a look of regret.

Tears sprang to her eyes, and she brushed them away.

"My apologies, didn't mean to upset you," Bill said. "The bedrooms are right this way."

Following Bill, Bets cleared her throat and moved ahead. The bedrooms looked fine. They'd use the smallest one to hide their stash of cash.

She pulled Zerk aside in the hallway. "I like it. What do you think?"

He kissed her forehead. "For the right price, I think we should take it."

"We probably don't have to worry about rent money," she whispered.

He broke into a smile. "That's right. We lucked out the other night. Let's do it."

They found Bill standing in the kitchen, looking over the water.

Zerk said, "How much were you thinking of charging for rent?"

"One thousand dollars a month," Bill said. "With one condition, that my mother can come by and visit anytime. She likes to bring her friends over from time to time to play cards. Seeing eagles soaring and catching salmon cheers her up."

Her stomach sank. There was no way they could let his mom into the house. They couldn't have visitors prying and perhaps discovering the money.

"I'm sorry, it's beautiful, but that won't work."

Zerk said, "We like the place and money's not an issue, but we need our privacy. We'll find another house to rent."

"I knew it was a strange request," Bill said, rubbing his temples. "Tell you what, why don't you rent it? I want the right people in here, and you seem like trustworthy folks. I'll tell my mother she can't bring her friends over for card games anymore." He shrugged. "It wasn't that often anyway. What do you say? Are you interested?"

Bets and Zerk exchanged a quick look and nodded to each other.

"Sounds great," Bets said. "When can we move in?"

Bill dug out a key and handed it to her.

"Today. Let's go the office, and I'll have you sign a lease."

Zerk said, "Bets," and clapped a hand over his mouth. "I mean, Jasmine, let's walk the dog around the property and check it out."

She gave him a scalding look for using the wrong name.

"Yes, Phil, let's do that."

"I'll let you lock up then, after you take a look around. Meet me at my office in say thirty minutes? That'll give me time to draw up the lease."

"We'll see you there," Bets said.

15

JAS

When Phil's credit card was declined at Starbuck's, Jas used the last bit of cash in her wallet to buy coffee and sandwiches for Phil and Dan. She was too nervous to drink or eat anything herself. Dan offered to pay, but she'd declined. He was already going overboard by driving them north and paying for gas.

Sitting at a long table and opening her laptop, she went online. She checked her emails, where were mostly ads and solicitations for political campaigns she'd never signed up to support. But there in the middle of the messages was an email from her father.

"Stay safe. Thanks for trying to come up with the money. Don't worry about me. I've had a good life."

Tears blurred her vision. If only her father could live forever. It hurt too much to think of him not being alive. Who would she call when things got her down? He'd always been there for her on the other end of the phone line or at home when she knocked on the door.

Her eyes fell on a fraud alert email from her bank.

Someone had tried to change the online password for her bank account. Her fingers tingled as she closed the laptop. The damn thieves were taking everything they could. First the cash in the car, then the credit cards and now attempting to hack into her bank account.

She stood. "Guys? We need to get going. I want to find a Mountainside Bank branch and withdraw my money before they drain that account. I have my passport, so I'll use that for identification. Phil, you should let your bank know too."

He closed his laptop. "Already did."

"What will you do with the money?" Dan asked.

"Keep it from the thieves, and I can reimburse you for gas and expenses."

Dan and Phil got up, tossing their cups in the trash.

Maybe she could still drive him if they recovered the money and wrapped this up in time. It was a six-hour trip from her dad's place to Tijuana. If she had to drive all night to get him there on time, she would.

An hour later, they pulled into a Mountainside Bank branch parking lot outside Salem, Oregon.

Jas got out. "You guys wait here. I'll withdraw my money and warn them about the people who are impersonating me."

Inside the bank, elevator music droned. She stood behind two women, tapping her foot and grinding her molars at how the thieves foiled her plans.

A middle-aged woman in front of her glanced at Jas and raised her eyebrows, eyeing the purple skort.

"I know, not everyone can pull this look off, right?" Jas said.

When she got to the teller window, Jas pulled out her passport and held it up. "My name is Jasmine Bucker, and I'm here to withdraw the money in my bank account."

The teller pushed his glasses up on his nose. "I see. I'll need to take a closer look."

Jas pushed her passport toward the teller through an opening in the plexiglass.

The older man examined the document and pushed it back to her.

"I'm afraid this isn't valid identification. It's expired. Do you have a driver's license?"

Jas studied the passport, which had expired last week. She'd forgotten to renew it amid the news of her dad's health crisis. Before she could get into Mexico, she'd have to get a temporary enhanced driver's license. What a hassle.

"I lost my driver's license. Can't you make an exception and use the passport?"

"We must follow rules," he said with a sniff. "If not, a system collapses in on itself."

Jas frowned. She'd been a stickler for following rules. All that was in the past.

"It's my money, and I want it before someone pretending to be me gets it."

The teller frowned. "You need current photo identification to make a withdrawal. I'm sorry I can't help you."

He reached below the counter and stared, watching every move.

Turning on her spike-less golf-shoed heel, she marched out the door.

She ran to the tow truck, where the engine was running, and hopped in, slamming the door shut. She leaned over Phil to turn off loud rock music and said to Dan, "Drive fast. Get out of here. They wouldn't give me my money."

Dan hit the gas and squealed out of the parking lot, heading for I-5 North.

"Are we still going to Millersville?"

Phil nodded. "Yes, we are. The thieves are in that town. They stayed overnight at a place called Two Rivers Resort."

"Sounds nice," Dan said. "Maybe we can stay there."

"We'll see," Phil said.

"I'll pay for it," Dan said.

"We may need you to do that," Jas said, "given how the thieves are chipping away at our financial stability with credit cards and trying the bank accounts. So, thanks. You'd think they'd be satisfied with what they have. Isn't it enough? Why are they wanting more?"

She cringed. She'd considered the plan to help her father but not the consequences of stealing. The robbers were ruthless, taking what they could. Her boss Andy was known to have a temper. What if he hunted her down and hurt the others?

Phil's voice broke into her thoughts. "I've been tracking their online searches using our phones, and the results are quite interesting."

"What do you mean?" she said.

"They looked for a restaurant that serves a good breakfast and went to a place called Dad's Diner."

Dan said, "What else?"

"They searched for vacant lots for sale, home builders, and hardware stores, where they bought duct tape, heavy-duty plastic, tin foil, chains and padlocks, and an outdoor security camera, but not the type that connects to the internet. The more we know about them, the better prepared we'll be to surprise them when we meet up and take back what was ours."

"Excellent," Jas said. "We're doing this for my dad. We'll get it back."

Phil said, "Dan, can we use your phone while you drive? Jas and I will use Google Images and try to find the thieves.

They used what sounded like nicknames, so that might help."

"What'd they look like?" Dan said. "Just curious."

"The woman had a black mole on the side of her nose," Jas said. "She was wearing a blond wig." Jas picked it off the floor and held it up. It had dirt streaks on it, but she'd wear it as a disguise when they caught the thieves.

"The guy stood out," Phil said. "He had a dragon tattoo on his neck, with the head, eyes and claws with long talons. I'd know that tattoo anywhere."

"Use my phone," Dan said, "and tell me what you find. It'll keep me awake driving. We've got about five hours to go, depending on traffic."

16

BETS

After signing the lease, using Jasmine and Phil's names, Bets pushed stacks of twenty-dollar bills across Bill's desk.

"There's first and last month's rent," she said.

"A bunch of twenty-dollar pretty puppies," Zerk said.

Bill counted the cash and cocked his head. "You sure you want to pay in cash?"

"We do," Zerk said, picking at a grease stain on his pants from breakfast.

"It makes it a bit difficult," Bill said, "and might look suspicious. I like to stay on the straight and narrow, you know?"

Zerk said, "We totally agree with you, don't we hon?"

Bets nodded and chimed in. "Absolutely, a hundred thousand percent. But you see, we're dealing with a strange set of circumstances. We came into money from my dear auntie. It was left to me in cash with the stipulation I spend it for something that would make me happy. And this would make me happy, renting your mother's house and paying you to build our home. Is there any way you could find it in your heart to accept payment in cash?"

Bill drummed his fingers on the desk.

"It's not how I like to run my business, but I'll make an exception for you. Maybe I'll use it to buy a beach house on Cedar Island. You promise me the authorities won't come looking for me, and I'm not going to be in trouble for taking this?"

Bets shook her head. "No way that'd happen. We're just innocent people trying to spend my great-aunt's gift money." She shrugged. "I have no idea why she left it in cash and didn't have it in the bank like everyone else. But who am I to question a gift?"

Bill tapped the desk. "Makes sense. I guess I won't question it either."

He stood and walked them to the door.

"Remember, keep the sump pump running at all times. Don't turn it off, or the basement might fill with water and flood the house when it rains."

"You bet," Zerk said, shaking hands with Bill.

Bets waved. "Thanks now."

As they left the office, Bets said to Zerk, "I hope his mom won't come waltzing in the place like she owns it."

"She won't," Zerk said. "Don't worry about it. Want to stop at the pub we saw? I'm thirsty."

Bets smiled at him as she climbed in the driver's seat.

"We shouldn't go out in public, but why not? We'll celebrate finding a place to rent and having a house built. But after this, we've got to stay home and out of sight. I don't want anyone finding out where we're from or that we have money. They might put together the pieces. Heist outside Vegas and a new couple with cash in town. Promise?"

He buckled his seat belt. "Promise. Last beer out for the rest of my life."

Her jaw ached with worry when he said that because Zerk loved to go to bars, brag about his exaggerated accomplishments and hang out with the guys. It was only a matter of time until he broke his word and found his way to a watering hole where he'd make instant friends. He'd leak enough of the truth that they'd risk being arrested.

As she drove toward the pub, she put a hand over his. "I mean it, this time we have to keep our word and not brag or blab."

He squeezed her hand. "You don't have to remind me. I'm a new man. I can keep a secret."

Pulling up in front of the Brown Lantern, she wasn't sure. When old, comfortable habits called, you overlooked the risks. She knew because she'd sworn last month to stop living a life of crime and go straight. But when the opportunity presented itself two nights ago, she couldn't resist. Now, with a once-in-a-lifetime haul, she and Zerk would leave that behind and start over.

Inside the Brown Lantern, they sat on bar stools and ordered local Mac & Jack's beers. The female bartender set chilled glasses down with an amber liquid inside. Bets took a sip. It tasted like caramel.

"This is good, isn't it?"

"I like it." Zerk drained his glass and said to the bartender, "I'll have another."

When his second drink came, they ordered Reuben sandwiches.

Zerk said, "While we wait, I'll go have a smoke."

He went out the back, carrying his beer.

Bets could see him chatting with a few men. Zerk had tried to quit smoking last month, but that hadn't lasted long.

So far, all their good intentions had gone down the drain. Maybe they weren't meant to be good people. She wondered if it was possible to switch sides and become model citizens. She'd fight like hell to try. It was the only way they'd survive from now on, by appearing to be who they weren't.

While Zerk smoked, she looked around. She'd been so wrapped up in herself, she hadn't taken in her surroundings. Wood paneling on the walls served as a backdrop to framed photos of athletes. A bicycle with fat tires hung from a rafter, the type her dad used when she was young and they went out for family bike rides. After that, her mom moved her to the country, where they lived in isolation, tending to pigs and chickens.

The young bartender, who had tattoos down her arms, served their sandwiches.

Bets glanced toward the back patio. She waved her arms, but Zerk didn't notice. He was too wrapped up in whatever discussion was going on with three other men. She hoped he'd keep his mouth shut about their secrets.

When she bit into her sandwich, her mouth was having a party. Buttered toast, salty pastrami, sauerkraut. Zerk would appear when he wanted to. He was a grown man, not a pet on a leash.

Bets turned and looked out the front window to the car, where Mimi was barking in the front seat at passersby. The window was down three inches, and the day was overcast and cool. The dog would be fine until they finished eating.

"I'll have another beer," she said to the bartender.

Her tattooed arms reminded her of Zerk's dragon tattoo and how he needed to get that removed so no one would recognize him. They couldn't have a clean slate if the couple in the car fingered them.

Zerk slid onto his bar stool and wolfed down a bite.

"Man, that's good." He smacked his lips. "Nice guys out back. We had a few laughs."

He dove into his sandwich again.

Bets looked at her half-empty plate. What he'd said made her lose her appetite.

"What did you tell them?"

"Nothing much, just how we hit the jackpot, what with your uncle's cash, and we're taking early retirement."

Food knotted in her stomach, and she felt nauseous.

"It wasn't my uncle, you idiot, I said it was my great aunt at the contractor's office. We need to stick to the same story, or people will get suspicious."

"Whatever," he said with his mouth full.

"And don't mention our cash, or people will come sniffing around for handouts. Keep your head on straight from now on, or you'll ruin our chances of sitting on our biggest haul ever."

Her blood rushed through her ears, and her pulse pounded. Sometimes he drove her to the outer limits of tolerance. Although she loved him, he tested those limits from time to time, like right this minute.

"All finished?" the bartender said.

"Yes," she managed to say.

"Care to take it with you?"

"No, it was good, but something ruined my appetite."

"Not me," Zerk said, reaching for her plate. "I'll eat it."

While Mimi barked in the car, Bets had an urge to run out of the pub and leave Zerk behind. By shooting off his big fat mouth, he'd let people know they had cash, which was dangerous. What had he done?

17

JAS

As Dan drove, heading north on the freeway, Phil and Jas hunted for images of the thieves, who had pretended to be police officers.

Phil turned Dan's cell phone toward Jas. "Does that look like her?"

"Nope. We're not getting very far, are we?"

She thought about what the thieves called each other. "Bets could stand for Betsy."

"That's a nickname for Elizabeth," Dan said. "My mom's sister is called Betsy."

Jas threw Phil a look. "Try Betsy and criminal."

"Nope, nothing."

"Narrow it down more," she said. "Try Elizabeth, robbery, Las Vegas."

"Bingo," Phil said, turning the Google images search to her.

"That's her," Jas said, "without the blond wig. Last name?"

"Ringer."

Jas leaned over to Dan, "Does that name sound familiar? Elizabeth Ringer?"

He kept his eyes on the road. "It doesn't. But I don't remember customers' names. I just tow their cars and take their money." He chuckled. "Tow, take, and save for a rainy day, that's what my mom says."

As if on cue, raindrops hit the windshield.

"Let's see if we can find the man," Phil said. "Then I'll look up their criminal records, if I can find them. Bets called him by a nickname. What was it? Zap? Zug?"

Jas tapped her lips. "She called him Zerk. Could be part of his last name."

Phil typed while he talked. "I'll put in Zerk, robbery, Las Vegas, Elizabeth Ringer."

"Bingo. There's his dragon tattoo." He showed the phone to Jas and then Dan.

"Big tattoo," Dan said.

"Must've hurt to get it," Phil said. "Not what I'd want to do."

Jas resisted the urge to lean down and scratch her legs. A red rash from brushing up against poison oak was spreading. It took all of her self-control not to rip at her skin and open the blisters that were forming.

"His name is Mark Zerkowitz," Phil said. "Now we're getting somewhere."

Jas smiled. "We're stalking our prey and armed with information. We'll catch them off guard."

"Look at this. The photo shows them at a charity softball game and a Boys & Girls Club auction."

"I guess they're not all bad," Dan said.

"Can you look at their criminal records?" Jas said.

Phil's fingers flew, typing fast. "Nope, looks like they were never convicted. Tell you what though, I'll see if I can tap into their phones and listen to their conversations. That'll put us ahead in the game."

Jas stared. "You know how to do that?"

"I do." Phil looked shy and humble, but he was the cornerstone of operation Get Dad's Money Back.

"It's like a game," Dan said, driving past the city of Olympia.

"A potentially deadly one," Jas said. "Dan, are you sure you want to help us? It might get ugly, confronting professional criminals."

"I'll be fine, I've seen a lot over the years. Don't worry about me."

Jas tugged on Phil's arm. "I just remembered I saw part of their license plate. I think it had ZRK in it."

"Which would fit with the name Zerk," Dan said, honking his horn at a car that cut too close in front of the truck.

Phil said, "I can't find anything online, but I'll keep a look out when we hit town for a dark four-door older sedan with a license plate with ZRK. They might've ditched the car by now."

18

BETS

Bets parked the car in front of Cabin Eight at Two Rivers Resort. She hadn't seen any rivers, but then again, they hadn't hiked on the trails. Glaring at Zerk because he'd mentioned coming into money to the guys at the pub, she wanted to shake him. But that wouldn't help. He was who he was.

He grinned, ignoring her foul mood, and slapped the hood of the car.

"Okay, honeybee, let's get the car loaded and move into our new deluxe digs."

"I'll load faster than you can," she said.

"Challenge accepted. The race is on."

They huffed and puffed, hauling trash bags filled with cash into the sedan.

Zerk said, "Now the suitcases, and then we'll be set."

He whistled while he worked, and she kept a lookout by the car, guarding the cash. He'd been in a cheerful mood since stopping at the pub. It turned out he'd been thirsty not only for beer but for an audience. She hoped his tendency to be the class clown wouldn't be their downfall.

He closed the cabin door and threw the key in the air, catching it.

"Why don't you return the key, and I'll meet you up there in a minute?"

"Sure."

She glanced at the office but had a feeling he was up to something. She'd have to keep an eye on him. If he took the money and left her, she'd be totally screwed.

"You know what? Why don't you drive me over, and I'll drop off the key?"

She hopped in and slammed the car door before he could say anything. She gripped the cabin key, and her fingers turned white. A thought occurred to her. What if they ended up hating each other every minute, and they were trapped in a house they were building with no escape? What had they done to themselves by taking that money?

When she turned in the key, the owner said, "Leaving us so soon?"

"We found a place to rent."

His thick eyebrows went up.

"That was fast. If you don't mind me asking, what's in those bags you keep moving around? They looked heavy. Most people would've left it in their car."

Bile rose in her throat. The Reuben sandwich twisted in her gut. Nosy people like the resort owner brought bad luck.

"Old magazines of my mother's. They were precious to her, so I have them as keepsakes. Everyone has their quirks, don't they?" She laughed.

The owner studied her, as if something was wrong with her. "I guess whatever makes you happy. I keep old issues of *Consumer Reports*, but I don't carry them with me where ever I go."

Zerk honked the horn, and Mimi barked in the car.

"That's my ride, got to go," Bets said, hurrying out the door.

"That guy was nosy," she said, getting in the car. "Everyone wants to know our business."

Zerk shrugged as he drove through a grove of evergreen trees toward town.

"You're too worried. Relax. It's time to enjoy ourselves. We've got it made."

She frowned. He was easy-going, and that's what attracted her to him in the first place. She pulled down the visor to check her teeth and make sure no pastrami was stuck. Behind them, the teenage son of the resort owner pedaled his bike, keeping a steady pace.

She slapped the visor up and turned to get a better look.

"That kid is tailing us on a bike."

Zerk laughed. "Come on, like that would happen."

Patting his shoulder, she said, "I mean it, speed up and lose him."

He glanced in the rear-view mirror.

"You're right. Hold on, Mimi, here we go."

Their dog barked as he floored it and left the kid in the dust.

At the waterfront house, they lugged in the trash bags and suitcases.

Bets pulled out the tin foil they'd bought earlier in the day.

"I'll put this on the windows while you set up the security camera."

He rested his hands on his hips.

"Don't you think it's carrying things too far? Tinfoil on the windows?"

"This is not a time to argue with me, not after you bragged about having money at the bar. This is a time for a low profile. After three years, maybe we'll relax a bit. But we can never mention the money to anyone."

He looked her in the eye, which always got to her, right down to tingling her toes.

"You're totally right," he said. "I'm sorry. My mouth got ahead of my brain."

"As it always does. And who saw the opportunity to take the cash? It was me, wasn't it?"

He flashed her one of his winning smiles, and his brown eyes twinkled. "We're in this gorgeous place," he turned around with his arms open wide, "with a view of the water, all because of your sharp eyes."

She swatted his arm and smiled. "Let's get back to work."

She taped tinfoil to the windows, humming as she worked. She was almost finished when Zerk brought in three blue plastic trash cans with lids.

"I'll put these in the smaller bedroom and move the money into them, so it'll be easy to grab what we need to pay rent or for work on our house."

"Did you check the security camera to make sure it's working?"

She felt like she had to check on him and follow up on forgotten details. But he didn't always appreciate it.

"It's not working. We need to get someone out here to fix it."

"I don't want anyone poking around in our private space."

"Let me handle them," he said. "We need Wi-Fi too. Bill's mom didn't need it. But we do."

A key rattled in the lock.

A woman in her mid-seventies came in, followed by three older women.

"Here we are, home sweet home," the woman said

before spotting Bets and Zerk in the kitchen. "What are you doing in my house?"

Bets and Zerk held up their hands.

"We rented the place," Bets said, "from your son today."

The woman arched an eyebrow. "I'm sure Bill would've mentioned it. You're squatters. What're you doing in my home? Tinfoil on windows? Take it down at once."

Bets said in a low voice to Zerk, "Call her son, let her talk to him. We need to get them out of here."

While Zerk dialed, Bets went over to the woman.

"I'm Jas, and this is my wonderful husband Phil. We love your place, and we're going to take good care of it."

The woman squinted at Bets. "You're going to grow pot, aren't you? You'll paint the walls black and ruin my beautiful house."

Mimi the dog came running in. She ran up to Bill's mother and sniffed her ankle.

Bill's mom yelped.

Zerk glided across the floor to the woman, who sat on the leather couch with her three friends. Nothing seemed to disturb Zerk, and Bets appreciated that.

He held out the phone. "Your son would like to speak with you."

She took the cell. "Yes?"

Bill's voice sounded loud and firm to Bets.

His mother nodded. "Uh huh. I understand. Fine."

She hung up. "My son says he rented the house to you. He reminded me," she dabbed her eyes, "that I don't own the house. He does. When I moved out, I told him he could do what he liked with it."

Bill's mother looked from Zerk to Bets. "Can I have one last game of cards with my friends and enjoy the view? Please?"

"One last time?" a woman in a long skirt and Birkenstock sandals said.

Zerk said, "As long as it's a quick card game, and then you're out."

Bets shot him daggers with her eyes. This was not okay. It could be a disaster.

"Thank you, absolutely, yes," Bill's mother said, pulling a card table out of the entry closet and setting it up. "One game of Hearts, and we'll be out of your hair. My name is Lucinda, by the way."

"Nice to meet you, Lucinda," Bets said, doing her best to be polite. She didn't want word to get back to the builder that they'd been unkind to his mother. She'd put up with Lucinda if it meant moving into the house of her dreams as soon as possible.

An hour later, a gray-haired woman said, "I'm shooting the moon!"

The laughing and cackling were nothing like Bets had heard before. Who were these joyous older women, and why were they so happy? Were they on drugs?

Lucinda said, "My throat is dry. Might you have some brandy or bourbon? Just a sip would quench my thirst."

Ms. Birkenstocks chuckled. "A tumbler full would be better."

Bets rolled her eyes and said to Zerk, "What do you think? Do you want to share your Maker's Mark?"

When he hesitated, Ms. Birkenstocks said, "Maker's Mark, wouldn't that be a treat? We don't get that at Chandlery Square for Happy Hour. Would you be willing to crack open a bottle and share a wee drop?"

Zerk said. "Whatever the ladies want."

Soon, the ladies were playing cards, laughing and gossiping, while Bets and Zerk sipped beverages at the breakfast bar. Bets envied their comradery and wished for a day when she could make friends.

Right now, she couldn't trust anyone but Zerk. She'd protect their secret past. If she let her guard down, someone would report them to the police, and they'd be arrested for the commercial laundry robbery. She hoped the money wouldn't make her a prisoner in her home.

19

JAS

Driving through Seattle, Dan swerved to avoid a fast-moving BMW cutting across lanes.

"Man, drivers here are jerks," he said, hunched over, clutching the wheel tight. "Glad it's only three more hours to Millersville."

Phil was on his laptop with his mobile hotspot, tracking the thieves.

Jas said, "What I wouldn't give for a decent meal and a hot bath now."

"I'm fine," Dan said. "I'm having an adventure."

She said, "If we get the money back, I'll treat you to a celebratory drink."

"Cool," Dan said, "and do I get part of the cash?"

Jas frowned. She'd hoped Dan wouldn't bring it up, but not sharing some of the money would be taking advantage of him and would confirm his mother's fears. She looked at Phil, who shrugged.

"Without my truck, you wouldn't have followed them."

"That's true," Jas said. "Why don't we set aside two-hundred-thousand dollars for my dad's treatment and split what's left equally? Phil, is that okay with you?"

Phil said, "I went along with this idea of yours because I like you, and I was hoping to get closer to you. You were desperate to help your dad, and I was bored at my job. I couldn't stand one more day of writing code. So, yeah, it sounds fine. But let's make sure we don't get killed or kill anyone else."

"We're thieves with a conscience?" Dan said. "Count me in. No one dies, we split the money, and your dad has hope. Maybe I'll retire early and leave the towing to my mom."

Just then, a yellow Ferrari raced past the truck in the middle lane of the freeway.

"Jeez," Dan said, "that looks like my mom's car."

He looked at the license plate. "It is her car."

When he honked three times, the Ferrari honked back and paced them, before falling behind.

Dan's phone rang.

When Phil answered it, a woman said, "Let me talk to my son."

Phil held out the phone so Dan could hear. "Okay, he's listening."

"He'd better be, this traffic sucks. Okay, Dan, how're you doing?"

"Fine, Mom, but you didn't have to follow me."

"You know how I hate to be left out."

Dan nodded and mouthed to Jas and Phil, "Told you so."

He said, "I thought you might show up. What's your plan?"

"Wherever you're going, I'm going with you. I told Lettie the neighbor to watch the ranch. Tim's Towing is taking our calls until we get back. Now let me in on where we're going and what we're up to."

Jas and Phil looked at each other with raised eyebrows. She held up her hands in surrender. This wasn't what she'd planned when she set out to steal money, but she'd go along with it. They needed Dan's truck to finish the job.

"Who's there with you? Speak up and introduce yourselves."

Jas took the phone. "Hello, this is Jasmine. I'm here with a friend named Phil, and your son has been kind enough to drive us."

"Dan," said his mother, "how much did these strangers take you for? How much are you in the hole? Jasmine and Phil, if you take advantage of my son, I'll hunt you down and hurt you."

Jas cringed.

"Ma, I only paid for gas," Dan said. "Their money was stolen, and their credit cards got hacked."

His cheeks were red. "Ma, come on, you're treating me like a kid. You're embarrassing me in front of my friends."

Jas said, "We like your son, and we won't take advantage of him. This whole trip is because I'm trying to help my dad. He's sick." A tear rolled down her cheek. "I promised to pay for his treatment, but my money was stolen."

"Let's talk about it later," Dan said. "We're going to Two Rivers Resort in Millersville. Look for Cabin Eight. We'll see you there."

"Any of you want to ride with me? It'll be faster."

Jas glanced at Phil, who looked like he was thinking about it. He'd told her he'd like to have a Ferrari one day.

Phil shook his head and said into the phone, "Thanks, but we're good. See you at the resort. The cabin is reserved under your son's name."

The yellow Ferrari took off and zoomed ahead.

"Guess we'll be sharing beds tonight," Jas said.

"You can sleep with my mother," Dan said. "She snores, and so do I."

Phil cleared his throat. "I do too."

"It looks like it's earplugs for everyone," Jas said.

The Ferrari was a yellow dot in the distance.

Nothing was going according to her original plan.

In a few hours, they'd be in the same town as the thieves who took their money.

Her stomach churned with trepidation.

20

BETS

Twenty minutes later, Bets was tired of babysitting the card players in the living room. She needed to be alone with Zerk to plan their next steps. The first thing she wanted to do, after loading the cash into the trash cans in the small bedroom, was get Wi-Fi set up. She felt cooped up without being able to surf online whenever she wanted to.

"I've had enough of this," Zerk whispered to her, rising from a bar stool. "I'm going in the study to organize our stuff."

She tugged on his hand. "Don't do that now, it's too risky. I'll get rid of them."

"Good luck," he said, glancing at the women. "They're glued to those chairs."

Bets checked the time on the phone she stole and clapped her hands.

"Five o'clock. You don't want to miss dinner at Chandlery Square, do you?"

Bill's mom rose, "I had no idea how late it was. We'd better get going."

Ms. Birkenstocks slapped her cards down.

"Thank you for hosting us, dear," Bill's mom said. "What was your name?"

Bets' heart fluttered. Even though her life of crime called for it, she was a reluctant liar. "Jasmine, like the flower."

Bill's mom came over and wrapped her in her arms, patting her back. Bets almost melted. She'd grown up without much maternal affection, and this was offered like a warm casserole right out of the oven. Bill's mother smelled like lilacs, coffee, and brandy, pleasantly mingling together.

She gave Bill's mom a feeble pat on the back and stepped away.

"Thanks for coming by, but remember, this is your last time. You wouldn't want to walk in on my husband and I doing the hokey-pokey in the living room, would you? That would embarrass all of us."

Bill's mom said, "We'll try to remember."

She chortled and her friends joined in, sounding like a bunch of birds.

"Come on girls, let's leave the lovers alone."

Bets saw them out and locked the door.

Zerk came into the living room. "You cleared them out?"

She smiled. Of the two of them, she was the smoother operator socially. She knew how to manipulate people more than Zerk.

She flipped the card table on its side and folded the legs while he collapsed the chairs and stored them in the front closet.

"We need Wi-Fi," he said, "and groceries, for starters."

She said, "We're idiots about setting up Wi-Fi. We never did get it work at the apartment, so I'll hire someone. After that, no strangers in the house."

Bets saw an eyeball peering in through a gap in the tin foil.

She pointed. "Someone's looking in."

Zerk moved to the door and opened it, poking his head out.

"Who is it?" Bets said, going over and hoping it wasn't the cops. Although she and Zerk were suspected of committing several crimes, the police couldn't pin anything on them. In the last year, they'd gotten away with robbing a 7-12 store with a cap gun, and holding up a drycleaner and clearing out the till at a Scoopa Joe's ice cream shop. It wasn't big money but enough to get by until the next job.

Zerk said, "It's the kid from the cabins."

"Come on, really?" Bets followed him outside. The kid was leaning against the side of the house. "What're you doing here?"

"I'm bored. I saw your car in front of The Brown Lantern. Wish I was old enough to go in there."

"Listen, kid," she said, "it's not all that exciting, so get over it."

Zerk nodded. "She's right. Being grown-up isn't all you think it is, so enjoy your life until you have to work for a living."

The kid said, "Can I have some tequila? I saw bottles in your car, it looked like you had extra."

Zerk clapped him on the back. "Nice try, but get out of here. We're enjoying our honeymoon, and we don't want any stinking company. Beat it."

The teenager got on his bicycle and pedaled off.

When the coast was clear, Bets said, "Good grief, we came here for peace and quiet, and all we're getting is visitors. I'll see if we can get an IT person out here. I miss having the internet." She shivered. "It's chilly, isn't it? Must be the breeze blowing?"

"We'll buy jackets tomorrow," he said as they went inside and locked the door.

Bets got on the stolen phone and searched for a local company that could set up the internet.

When the phone rang, she was startled. She hoped it wasn't the father of the young woman who owned the phone. That had been a hassle, getting him off the line last time.

Bets shook her head. People were too emotional, and it ruined their lives. That's why she and Zerk were perfect for their jobs. Get in, get out, no regrets. Leave your emotions at the door. If you didn't, you might overlook a critical detail and make a mistake.

"Hello?" she said, in a neutral tone. She wasn't going to be tricked into telling anyone who she was. She'd have used her own cell phone for the recent searches except she'd run out of data on their limited plan.

A man said, "I'm calling from Connectivity Plus, and we saw you were on our website. Is there anything we can do to help you?"

Bets gestured to Zerk, who was standing nearby, with a what the heck gesture. How could a company track her internet searches? She cleared her throat to buy time and decided it was possible her search might've been visible to all-powerful tech-types in business. She didn't know much about computers, but it sounded feasible.

"Yes, I'm looking for someone to set up Wi-Fi in our house."

"You're in luck. We're calling to offer you a one-time deal for an in-home visit, where we'll bring along the equipment you'll need and install it. Would tomorrow be a good time?"

Bets tilted her head. Something was fishy about this one-time offer. But they did need internet at the house.

"How much would it cost? Can you bring a security camera with you that connects to our phones? We don't know how to do that. We brought an outdoor camera that isn't connected to the internet."

"Of course, we can do that for you as well. We'd be happy to provide the services, materials package, and installation for only one-thousand dollars."

Bets gasped. "That's way too much. We can't afford that."

Zerk whispered to her, "We can pay for it. Just tell them to get over here first thing tomorrow."

Every dollar spent was a dollar she wouldn't have later, so she wasn't going to throw money to the wind.

"How about five hundred dollars?" she said. "Would you do it for that? And show up first thing tomorrow morning?"

"Let me check with my supervisor. Would that be all right?"

Bets heard a rumbling noise in the background on his end and a horn honk, as if he was calling from a car or a truck.

"Yeah, check and see what they say," she said. "Tell them we'll be repeat customers if you provide good service."

"One moment, please," the man said.

Bets said to Zerk, "I've got them right where I want them. I'm a tough negotiator. No one rips me off."

The man came back on the line. "Five hundred dollars will be fine, and we look forward to solving your IT problems. Would ten o'clock tomorrow morning work for you? And what is your address?"

"That time will be fine. Hold on while I get the address." She said to Zerk, "What's the address? Go out and look."

Zerk came back and said, "1818 Hillside Drive."

Bets repeated it and added, "in Millersville."

"Yes, we'll see you there tomorrow."

She hung up, but something bothered her about the call. It seemed too easy.

21

———

JAS

At Two Rivers Resort on the edge of town, Dan parked by the office and went in to pay. Jas climbed out of the truck. Cool air crept into her skin and seeped into her bones. She shivered, rubbing her arms. Light rain started to fall, and a hush fell over the forest.

"Damp cold," she said to Phil. "I'm not dressed for this. I'm freezing."

"We need jackets," he said, jogging in place. "I wish we could go for a run now. That'd warm us up."

They often went for a run in the morning, but they'd skipped that the last few days.

"When this is over, I'd like to find a nice, quiet place to live." he said. "I might write a novel."

She snorted. "Everyone's writing a book these days."

"Mine would have car chase scenes. I'd base it on algorithms of what people like to read and put my computer skills to use. But I'd have to use a pen name."

Jas said, "I'll keep a low profile. I don't want my boss finding out where I am."

"Yoo hoo," a plump platinum blond woman called from a cabin in the woods, where a yellow Ferrari shimmered in the rain.

Jas waved. "Must be Dan's mother?"

"Has to be."

Dan came out of the office and started the truck. "Meet you there. Number Eight."

As they trod on a pine-needled path, Jas said, "I hope we can trust him and his mom."

"Well, he's gotten us this far."

She said, "We'll have to think up a plan in case he and his mom turn on us."

Watching Dan hug his mother made her miss her father, and a lump settled in her throat. When she'd convinced Phil to join her and use his car for the robbery, she'd told him it would be easy.

She had convinced him by saying, "I know the code to the safe, and when my boss is at his poker games. You've said you're fed up with your job, and I need the money to give my dad. You could start over with your own business. Why don't you help me this one time, and we'll never do it again?"

He had chewed on his lip. "I don't want to break the law or get thrown in jail. Can't you do this alone?"

Putting a hand on his arm, she had said, "I need a lookout and a bigger car than I've got. My old Carmen Gia wouldn't make it past the city limits. I thought you'd be into this, but I guess I was wrong."

He drummed his fingers on the blue tile kitchen counter.

"This could be your ticket out of the long work hours you've whined about," she'd said. "You'd minimize the risks by being there." She paused a beat before delivering her last pitch. "But if it's something you don't think you can do, I understand, and I'll do it on my own."

After a beat, he'd said, "All right, I'll do it."

Now, Dan's mom came over to them with a wide smile and open arms.

"If you're Dan's friends, you're friends of mine. My name is Roberta, but people call me Robbie."

As the woman enveloped Phil in a hug, light raindrops hit the maple leaves. Jas wished Robbie hadn't followed them. Adding another person to their group could increase the risk of failure.

Robbie let go of Phil and launched herself at Jas.

"And you, I hear good things about you."

"Nice to meet you," Jas said. Her words were muffled by the woman's embrace and her pillow-like breasts. This wasn't the sort of mother Jas pictured when they met Dan, and he'd described her. She'd imagined a wiry battle-axe. She found herself liking Robbie but wondered if they could trust her. Something about her was a little too perfect.

Dan clapped his hands. "Let's head inside and put together our plan for tomorrow."

Jas followed him into a one-room wood-paneled cabin. Off the kitchenette, and a sitting area with a sofa and two armchairs, were two double beds. She frowned. Sleeping in a room with three people who snored was not on her list of things to accomplish. Her drab one-bedroom apartment was looking good right now.

Dan pulled out a chair at a round dining table.

When the others sat, he said, "What's our next step? Phil, you're scheduled to meet with Bets and Zerk tomorrow at ten o'clock. But what do we need to do before that?"

Jas chewed on a fingernail and pondered how much Dan had changed. He was acting like a leader. He wasn't a timid tow truck driver anymore. Had he changed because his mother was here, or was it because he sensed they were closing in on their prey?

Phil said, "I think it'd be best if I got a haircut so they won't recognize me. I'll buy a hat and clear glasses to throw them off. We'll need to pick up the electronics gear tonight, like listening devices to hide in their home and a combination modem and router."

Jas said, "Also, I'd like to buy a raincoat and a fleece jacket. It's cold and wet."

"Same goes for me," Dan's mom said.

"Me too," Phil said.

Robbie said, "Wait, why are you chasing these people? What happened?"

"I took some money," Jas said, hoping she could trust Dan's mom, "from my boss at Consolidated Services."

Robbie frowned. "I've heard nothing but bad things about that company. It's a shady operation. Why did you take it?"

"To pay for my dad's healthcare," Jas said. "He's sick and needs medical treatment."

"Gosh, I'm sorry to hear that about your dad," Robbie said.

Phil said, "The thieves pulled us over on a two-lane road and pretended to be cops. They took the money, our driver's licenses, and phones, then they handcuffed us."

Robbie covered her mouth.

"A real police officer came by after that," Jas said, "and called your son, who drove us here."

"Why involve my son and get him into trouble? Couldn't you drive your car?"

Jas rubbed her temples, where a headache throbbed. Her stomach rumbled. If she didn't eat soon, she'd pass out.

"They removed the distributor," she said. "We had to get going and chase them, and Dan said he'd help us."

Robbie whistled. "This is a far different situation than I'd thought. Jas, you took money for the greater good, but it was still a crime. The thieves who stole your money meant for your dad were definitely in the wrong. Let me think about this for a minute."

Jas swallowed. Her ears clicked. She tapped her foot. If Robbie called the cops, she'd spend her life in prison. And so would Phil, who she'd talked into the caper.

Phil squirmed in his seat and crossed his arms.

Dan cleared his throat. "Mom, what're you thinking?"

Robbie said, "It was kind of you, son, to help these two. Maybe that was a mistake, or maybe not." She turned to Jas and paused, looking thoughtful. "I'll help you get the money back, for your father's sake."

Jas let out a whoosh of breath. Thank goodness. That was settled.

"I'm hungry," she said. "I propose we get a bite to eat before shopping for jackets and computer gear. The barber shops must be closed by now. Can you do that tomorrow morning?"

"That'll work," Dan said. "But before we do anything else, we need everyone at the table to agree to secrecy. No leaks, or one of us could die. Got it?"

As everyone nodded, Jas hoped they would all keep quiet. Four people offered a lot of variables. If any one of them made a minor mistake, it could ruin their mission.

"I'm fine with that," Robbie said. "But there's something I don't understand. Why we don't go in and take the money tonight or tomorrow? Why wait?"

Phil said, "We're not sure where they're keeping the money, and I want to be sure first, before we make a move."

Jas patted the table. "We'll take it step by step and plan everything out. No knee jerk reactions mean fewer mistakes. Understood?"

"Understood," Dan said, looking her right in the eye.

Jas turned to his mother, who was an unknown element. Come to think of it, she seemed like she could be a hot bed of impulsivity, with her fast car and her questions. "And you, Robbie?"

"Understood," Robbie said, "I can handle myself and keep secrets."

Jas caught a quick glance exchanged between Robbie and Dan. What secrets did they share that might get in the way of helping her father? She wouldn't let anyone stop her from reclaiming the money that was rightfully hers.

If she didn't drive her father across the border, as she'd promised, she'd never forgive herself.

22

BETS

Bets had a lot to do before the IT guy showed up tomorrow morning. First, they needed to buy rain coats. It was cool and rainy in the Pacific Northwest.

"Hey," she called across the house.

When he didn't answer, she walked to the small bedroom where he was tossing money into three thirty-two-gallon trash cans.

"Help me wrap a chain around each can," he said. "We'll lock them with padlocks."

"Sure thing."

She picked up a length of metal chain and wrapped it under the bottom and over the top of each can. She snapped a lock shut while he handled the other two. She smiled. Working together was one of their strengths. If it involved money, they were focused and on task with few words.

"Team Bets and Zerk, all the way, hey?" She smiled.

He grinned.

Stepping back, she crossed her arms and eyed the trash cans.

"But I'm not sure it'll stop anyone. Think about it, if someone wants to, they'll use an ax to break down the front door. They could haul the cans away, they've even got wheels, and cut the chains with bolt cutters. Maybe this isn't the best way to store the money."

Zerk wasn't always the brightest bulb. But he meant well. And he was a lot of fun, especially after he'd had a few beers.

"It's all about optics," he said, waving his hands in the air. "It'll scare them off."

He looked exasperated, which was to be expected, because they'd entered into one of their favorite arguments, with her playing the negative part while he was frustrated his wonderful idea wasn't appreciated. She counted to five, so she didn't react and make the situation worse.

"If anyone sees this," he said, "they'll decide it'll be too hard to haul these away or open them. They'll leave them alone."

"We hope. But hon, they look like something special is hidden inside, like locked treasure chests. We should've found a better way to stow the money. Like a home safe."

His face turned red.

"Absolutely not. You know how obvious that would look, to have a big safe sitting in this room? Besides, how would we even get a huge safe in here? We can do that when we're building a house, but for now, my idea is best. Do you have a better idea, my dear?"

She let her fisted hands drop to her sides and opened them to defuse the situation. Zerk was getting cranked out of shape. It wasn't good for his blood pressure.

"Let's stop arguing. I hate it when we do this."

He wiped his sweaty brow. "Me too."

She threw up her hands.

"I don't have a better idea. Let's just keep the bedroom door closed tomorrow when the IT guy shows up."

"I will, and we need to install a better lock on this door." He wrapped his arms around her. "What would you like to do next? Try out the beds? One at a time?"

She laughed. Talk about changing subjects, but it was a relief to leave the tension behind. "Let's start with the one in the master bedroom with the mirrored closet doors. Right this way, sir."

She pulled on his hand and led him down the hall. They deserved a good romp after all they'd been through in the last few days.

An hour later in bed, Bets sighed.

"We've still got the old magic going, don't we?"

"We do, I swear I saw fireworks going off at the end. They could make a movie about us, how we fight and we love hard."

She patted his arm and sat up in bed.

"We need to get to the shops before they close for the night. I need a rain coat."

"I thought you didn't want anyone to see us?" He stood and stretched. "We could order online and have it delivered."

"I want to stay out of sight, but we've got to do it, just this once. I can't go around shivering and getting wet until a coat arrives. What good is having money if I die from pneumonia?"

"That's a bit dramatic, don't you think?" he said. "We're going to live long, happy lives in this out of the way spot."

Driving to the store, he parked around the corner from Slocum Marine on Commercial Avenue and walked through the lobby of the Best Majestic Hotel.

"This place has outdoor gear for men and women," Bets said. "It's the only one around I could find."

Zerk glanced at a sign advertising a bar at the top of the hotel with a view of the San Juan Islands.

"Look, we can go up top after we shop. Sounds good, doesn't it?"

In a low voice, she said, "We can't go out like normal people anymore. We have to wait until things settle down. Maybe next year."

"Next year? No way I'll wait that long."

She arched her eyebrows and guided him into the store.

A middle-aged woman stood at the counter.

Bets said, "We're looking for rain coats and anything else you have to keep us warm."

Against a wall, a gas fireplace blazed. She went over to it and rubbed her hands together.

"Are you on a boat?" the woman said.

"Nope, just walking around, so far." Zerk gave Bets a look. "I wouldn't mind buying a boat. What do you think?"

Bets froze. A boat was tempting, but they needed to hoard their money for the future, not blow it all at once.

"The idea certainly has appeal," she said. "Let's talk about it later."

"We've got a boat for sale. A thirty-two-foot trawler-style power boat," the shop owner said.

"How fast does it go?" Zerk said with a smile. "Really fast?"

Oh man, Bets thought. He wants to go fast and run through our cash. Too bad she'd ended up in the role of putting on the brakes, the one who made sure they conserved their money. She wanted to be the fun babe, not the grumpy aunt scolding him.

The woman shook her head. "Our boat averages six

knots. It's not a fast boat, but it'll get you there, and you'll have time to see everything along the way."

He turned to Bets, looking like a kid with a new bike.

"I want a boat that flies across the water at super-fast speeds."

The woman said, "Those go-fast boats are more likely to hit logs and bend propellers."

"There's a lot to boating we don't know," Bets said. "We'd better hold off on buying a boat. Okay, back to jackets. What do you recommend?"

They picked out rain coats, fleece jackets, long underwear and hats.

"That should do it," Bets said.

As the woman went around the counter to ring up their purchases, Zerk studied a display of sunglasses. He tried on a pair and looked in the mirror.

"Got to get these, right, hon?"

"We're the largest Maui Jim sunglasses dealer in the region," the woman said. "With over one-hundred-sixty styles to choose from."

Zerk took another pair from the rack. "And these."

Bets walked over and picked out a pair. At this rate, their money would run out in a year if she didn't throttle back the impulse buying. But the sunglasses offered a fresh disguise, and people wouldn't remember their faces.

When she paid in cash, the woman's eyebrows shot up, but she accepted the money.

Handing Bets a bag loaded with their gear, the shop keeper said, "I'm Patty. Do you live in town? I haven't seen you before."

Her eyes grew wide. "We're new in town. We'll see you around."

She pulled Zerk away from the sunglasses display before he could find another pair to buy and headed out the door.

23

JAS

Leaving Frieda's Mexican restaurant after eating chicken enchiladas for dinner, Jas spotted Bets and Zerk exiting a store across the street. Her heart skipped a beat. She whipped around and gestured to Phil, Dan and Robbie, who were laughing, to keep quiet by putting a finger to her lips.

"It's the thieves," she said. "Turn around so they don't see us."

"Who?" Robbie said, looking around.

Dan put his hands on his mom's shoulders and spun her around. "Keep your voice low. It's the people who took Jas and Phil's money. We don't want them to notice us."

Thank goodness for Dan's cool-headed reaction, Jas thought. Robbie was the group's weak spot, with her flair for drama. They needed to grab the money and get out of town.

When she glanced back, Bets and Zerk were gone.

"We can cross the street now," she said, leading them into Slocum Marine.

Bells jingled at they walked in.

"Can I help you?" a middle-aged woman said. When she

smiled, her eyes crinkled with lines, as if she'd been out sailing and exposed to the sun for years.

"We're looking for rain coats and fleece jackets," Jas said.

"We're not from around here," Robbie said. "The damp cold is getting to me."

The shop keeper said, "Two people were just in here getting the same things."

Jas nodded.

"Are you new to town?" the woman said. "My last customers were. Do you know them?"

Jas shook her head. "Just passing through."

She pulled out a raincoat, thinking how keeping a low profile didn't fit Robbie at all. She was flash and pizazz, which was something Jas could use a bit more of. She marveled at how she could criticize, envy, and admire Dan's mother at the same time.

As Jas tried on a rain coat, Phil asked, "Do you have polypropylene long underwear? That would keep the ladies warm."

"I'm no lady," Robbie said with a loud laugh, "I'm a broad. Do you have my size?"

"Certainly," the shop clerk said.

They trooped out of the store wearing fleece jackets and heavy rain coats.

Jas and Robbie carried bags with long underwear.

Robbie grumbled, "I might not have come along if I'd known how chilly the month of March was in these parts."

"We didn't ask you to come along," Dan said.

Jas thought she heard an undertone in Dan's comment that he wished his mother had stayed on the ranch. But she was good company, Jas had to admit. Who knows, she might turn out to be an asset to the team.

Jas said, "Dan, thanks for paying for all this."

"Yeah, thanks, Dan," Phil said. "We'll pay you back."

Robbie pointed a finger at Jas and Phil. "Make sure you keep your promises."

Jas nodded. "We will."

A motion on her left caught her attention. Across the street, her boss, Andy, was peering into Dan's tow truck. They'd taken two vehicles to dinner because after they ate, Phil and Dan were going in the truck to pick up electronics gear.

Her heart raced, and she tugged on Phil's coat sleeve.

"My boss is across the street, looking in Dan's truck."

Phil's eyes grew wide. "What's he doing in town?"

Jas lifted her hands. "I don't know. Maybe he put trackers in with the money, and he's here because of Bets and Zerk? He must've noticed Dan's Nevada license plate."

She turned to Dan and Robbie. "Guys, we need to hide. My boss who I stole from is across the street."

When she pulled Phil into The Brown Lantern, Dan and his mom followed.

"We'll hide in here until he leaves," Jas said.

They sat at a table in the back and ordered beers, except for Robbie, who had a dirty gin martini with two olives.

"Nice place," Dan said, looking at the wood paneling, and photos, and sports jerseys on the wall. "I wouldn't mind owning a bar like this."

Her boss Andy walked in and ordered a beer at the bar.

Jas hid her face with her hand and stared at a coaster on the table. She elbowed Phil.

"Incoming on our right," she whispered.

Phil bent and fiddled with his shoe lace while Dan and Robbie studied the menu.

Time seemed to stand still as Andy passed them and went out to the smoking area.

Jas released a shaky breath.

"That was a close call. He's dangerous. We've got to get out of here."

Robbie set her martini down, grumbling that she hadn't finished it.

"Remember the plan?" Dan said. "Be discreet. I know it's hard for you to blend in."

Robbie said, "Blending in is for sissies. I'm more of a stand-out-and-notice-me kind of person."

Jas bit her lip. Robbie's tendency to attract attention meant Zerk, or Bets, or Andy might spot them at any minute. Jas had to think of a role for Robbie to take advantage of her strengths. She could be an entertaining distraction.

Jas stood and motioned to the door.

"Let's get out of here before he comes back."

"When we leave, turn left and keep your heads down," Phil said.

24

———

BETS

Light mist fell as Bets and Zerk went around the corner to their car and climbed in. Pulling on her new knit cap and fleece jacket, she leaned back and sighed.

"A moist climate is supposed to be good for your skin," she said. "But I didn't realize it'd give me goosebumps. What's summer going to be like? Windy and wet?"

Zerk pulled on his hat and studied himself in the rearview mirror, taking his sunglasses off and on.

"Doesn't matter. We picked a place to hide out, and we're building a house."

Cold fear crept into her chest. They were boxed in with no options. Why had they decided on Millersville? They should've evaluated other options. Talk about an impulsive decision, which was usually Zerk's specialty. She'd jumped in, feet first and regrets later.

Until now, they'd always left the option open of skipping town at a moment's notice and leaving everything behind except each other. She hoped their new attitude of putting down roots wouldn't come back and bite them in the butt.

She pointed out the window. "What do you think that guy is up to? Trying to steal a catalytic converter from that tow truck?"

Zerk took off his sunglasses and craned his neck.

"Don't think so," he said. "More like he wants to steal something inside the cab."

The man with slicked back hair swung around, looking right and left.

Bets and Zerk by reflex ducked down low in the car so they wouldn't be seen.

When the man pulled out a tire iron to smash a window, Zerk said, "I can't take it. I've got to do something. Tow truck drivers work hard. They shouldn't have their stuff stolen."

"Hey," Zerk said, hopping out of the car and going to the middle of the street. "Whatcha doing? You better not hurt that truck. Put the tire iron down."

Bets pulled on her rain jacket and stepped out of the car.

"Yeah, bug off. Don't break into hard-working people's vehicles. Shame on you."

The man stalked away.

Bets took Zerk's arm. "You tell'em, honey."

"You too, babe. We'll be the enforcers in town, keeping the streets safe."

She giggled. "Quite a change for us. Policing the city and stopping crime."

"Look out, a new squad is in town." He laughed.

She hugged him, thinking how long it'd been since they stood in the street and let loose laughing. They'd had too many money worries until now. His warmth seeped into her body as she leaned into him.

He let go and stepped back. "How about you stop at the grocery store, and I'll meet you back at the house? I want to walk around for a while, scope things out."

She nodded. They'd been together every minute since the robbery, and a break would be welcome.

"Sounds good, see you there. I have a hankering for Brussel sprouts, anything you'd like?"

He wrinkled his nose.

"Not those. We'll have to keep the windows open all night. They stink up the place."

"Just this once," she said. "Now do you want Cheetos? Doritos? Beer?"

"All of the above," he said with a smile. "You know me so well."

As she drove away, she noticed Zerk walking toward the Brown Lantern. The man didn't have a cautious bone in his body. She'd ream him out when he got home if he went in for a beer and talked with the guys in the smoking area out back. She'd be able to smell it on his clothes.

Bets went through the grocery store, loading up her cart and keeping her eyes down. Her hat was pulled low, and she was wearing the new sunglasses.

In the check-out line, a tall, gray-haired man in front of her turned around. "Excuse me, but I believe we met at Dad's Diner this morning? Harold Biggins."

He thrust out his hand like a welcoming committee.

"Hello," Bets said, shaking his hand. "We meet again."

Was everyone in this town on extrovert steroids? Had she entered a new dimension, where residents were brainwashed to be pleasant? It would be difficult to remain anonymous with people glad-handing and prying everywhere they went. Good intentions on the part of others meant meddling in her experience.

Back at the house, she walked in the door and found Mimi chewing on a sofa cushion.

"Bad dog," she said, pulling the cushion off the floor.

She shook a finger at Mimi. Now she'd have to go out in the daytime and get the upholstery repaired. It felt like events were spiraling out of control, and Zerk wasn't helping. She'd put money on his stopping at the Brown Lantern for a beer and entertaining his new pals, instead of taking a walk like he'd said. She'd grill him about it tomorrow.

"You should be ashamed of yourself," she told the dog, who whimpered and looked away.

A noise went off deep in the house, and Bets jumped.

Mimi yipped.

"I'll go see what it was," she said.

Searching for the source of the sound, she opened the basement door and went down the stairs.

Rain lashed the basement windows.

The sump pump was on.

Basement walls amplified the sound.

The relentless grinding noise reminded her of a jackhammer working nonstop.

"No way I can sleep with that racket."

When she flipped a switch, the sump pump became silent.

The dog waited at the top of the stairs.

She walked up the steps to the lovely home they'd lucked into renting.

"No one's going to tell us we don't know our way around house repairs, right, Mimi?"

25

JAS

The next morning, Jas woke up in a double bed at Two Rivers Resort. Her throat was dry. When she tried to turn over, a warm body blocked her way.

Next to her, Dan's mother mumbled in her sleep.

In the other bed, Phil was awake, checking Dan's phone while Dan snored.

Jas stared at the pine-paneled ceiling, trying to come up with a way to make Dan's mom less of a risk. When they made their final move on the house where Bets and Zerk were, what if Robbie knocked on the door and distracted the thieves? She could tell them she needed help with her broken-down car. Or, she saw a whale in the channel and to come outside and see it. That would take advantage of her outgoing nature and give her an important assigned role.

"Okay, everyone," Phil said, getting out of bed and standing in his boxer shorts. "I'll go take a quick shower. We've got a lot to do before ten o'clock. We're leaving in twenty minutes."

Dan yawned.

His mother groaned and stretched.

"I'll take the next shower," Dan said, sitting up. "I'll be quick."

By the time Jas stood in the shower, there was barely a trickle of lukewarm water coming out overhead. She washed her hair with the motel shampoo and got out. Poison oak blisters were all over her feet, and her ankles oozed.

It was chilly in the bathroom. The window and mirror were fogged. She turned on the heater. When it rattled and clanked, she turned it off.

Stepping into the main room, she said, "I'm ready."

Phil clapped his hands and assumed a leadership role, which was a good thing because they were depending on him for the reverse heist. Jas hoped he was a good actor, because their plan was risky, going right into the robbers' house. He could be found out at any minute.

"We're going in two cars," Phil said. "Robbie, I love your car, but it'll attract too much attention. We'll park it somewhere downtown away from Bets and Zerk's house. Remember, if anyone asks why you're here, say you're a tourist and you're going to go whale watching. Jas, you'll go with Robbie, and I'll go with Dan. We'll park a block from the house so as not to attract attention. First, Dan and I will go get buzz cuts."

Jas nodded. It was as good an idea as they could cook up on short notice. "What should Robbie and I do while you're getting haircuts and setting up their Wi-Fi?"

"Find out everything you can about the house they're in," Phil said. "Go to City Hall and look at blueprints for the building, noting any exit doors. We could drug the dog so it won't bark when we go in the house later to get the money, so buy natural peanut butter with no artificial sweeteners and Dramamine, less drowsy. That's supposed to work. I looked it up online. Keep a low profile and go to Safeway, bring us back food. And watch for Andy. Find out where he's staying. We'll meet here afterwards for a debriefing."

Phil was really stepping up his game, Jas thought. She hadn't known he had the potential to take charge, and she liked this side of him. Plus, he'd looked good in his boxer shorts this morning. She couldn't help but peek, even though she'd seen him in swim trunks with a group of friends at the pool.

"Okay, everyone got that?"

Jas and Dan nodded.

Robbie said, "Of course. That's not hard to remember."

"What time does City Hall open?" Jas said. "Do you know?"

Phil said, "I looked it up. Nine o'clock."

To Dan, he said, "Let's go. We'll let the girls lock up."

"We're not girls," Robbie called as the men left. "We're women who stick together, right?"

Jas smiled. "Right."

Getting into Robbie's low-slung car, Jas said, "Let's drive down Commercial and see if we can spot my boss."

Driving into town, the car rumbled and hugged the curves. It was the nicest, most expensive car Jas had been in, but she didn't feel envious. She enjoyed the smooth ride, but she'd rather buy a beach shack and settle down.

"I'm sorry your boss is after you," Robbie said.

Her face heated. She was ashamed of taking the money, but she didn't have an alternative. Where else would she have found two-hundred-thousand-dollars on short notice? The idea of robbing her boss occurred to her after Andy creeped her out and made unwanted moves.

When she came out of the bathroom at work, he was looming in the hallway, cornering her. He slapped her ass and whistled. When she told him off, he'd said she was too sensitive and probably going through that time of the month.

Her fists had tightened, and her jaw clenched.

"Don't ever touch me again."

Right then and there, she realized he had the money her father so desperately needed. Taking it would be payback for his misogynistic remarks and hallway harassment. She might as well take everything in the safe, rather than leaving part of it. If she was going to steal and take the risk of getting caught, she might as well go all out.

But now Andy had arrived in Millersville. She hadn't expected that to happen. She wondered if he'd installed a cell phone tracker app on her work phone, which she used as her personal cell. No sense in carrying two phones, she'd reasoned. Using one phone saved money. If so, he was tracking Bets and Zerk. Or he could've slipped a tracking device into the cash in the safe, or her purse. She wouldn't put it past him.

"He's a chauvinist pig," Jas said, "and my dad needs the money more than he does. I wanted to teach him a lesson and save my father at the same time."

Robbie pulled into a Walgreen's parking lot.

Jas sighed. Her dad needed her. She'd screwed up by losing the money. She'd failed him.

She fidgeted in the bucket seat. She hoped Phil would scope out the house this morning and bring back good intel for the final takedown. Watch out, thieves, we're coming after you.

After buying Dramamine, natural peanut butter, ear plugs, and two burner cell phones, one for Phil and one for her, they cruised down Millersville's main street, keeping an eye out for Andy. Like a rat scuttling down an alley, she saw him go into Dad's Diner.

She touched Robbie's arm. "My boss went in that restaurant. Let's wait until he comes out, and see where he goes."

Pulling into a parking spot, Robbie chuckled. "I'm enjoying being a secret spy."

"We may have a special assignment for you later. Can you impersonate a woman in distress with a broken-down car? Or pretend to see a whale and get Bets and Zerk out of the house while we go in and take the money?"

"I'll take the whale bit. This car is precious, and I don't want anyone pawing over it or looking under the hood. I'll get them away from the house for a few minutes."

"The timing will be tight. I'll talk it over with Phil first." Jas giggled. "Phil first, Phil first, it's hard to say fast a few times."

As they laughed, Andy walked out of the diner with a brown take-out box in his hand. He glanced at Robbie's car and walked over to them.

Jas pulled on her knit cap and slouched down, turning her head to the side and pulling her rain jacket hood up.

"If he comes over, you talk to him. Pretend I'm hungover and taking a nap."

"This is right up my alley, no worries. Leave it to me."

Robbie rolled down her window.

Andy said, "What a good-looking car. I've always wanted one of these."

"Not everyone can afford them," Robbie said. "She's my beautiful girl."

"I see you have Nevada plates. Where are you from?"

"Sin City, how about you?"

"That's where I'm from too. By the way, I was about to buy a car like this. It would've set me back more than ninety-thousand-dollars, except my employee stole my money. I'm looking for her. Have you seen a woman around thirty years old with short brown hair?"

"That description fits a lot of women. Can't say I have."

He patted the top of the car with a resounding whack.

"Here's my card. Let me know if you see her. There's a reward in it for you if you do. How's forty-thousand dollars sound? Her name is Jasmine Bucker, but she goes by Jas."

"I'll keep an eye out for her," Robbie said.

"I'd appreciate the help. Say, is everything okay with your friend over there?"

Jas was hot with the knit cap and rain coat on and the hood over her head.

Robbie patted her arm. "It's my niece. She's hungover and taking a nap."

"That's the worst. We've all had it happen. Take care."

Robbie rolled up the window and said to Jas, "He's walking away. I'll tell you when he's gone. He seemed like a nice fellow."

Her muscles tensed, and Jas bit back a scream of cuss words.

"He puts on a good act, but don't believe it. Just hearing his voice made me want to retch."

"I can see why. Does he have a girlfriend?"

"Look elsewhere, he's poison. You wouldn't want to go out with him."

"You never know," Robbie said. "I like long slicked back dark hair on a man. And he had a nice smile. He struck me as a genuine sort of person."

Jas frowned. Robbie wasn't listening to her and letting hormones take over. What if Robbie turned her in to Andy? She couldn't let that happen.

"You can sit up," Robbie said. "He's gone. Forty-thousand-dollars is a big reward. Maybe I should turn you in. I could use the money to pay off the mortgage on the ranch."

Jas felt like throwing up. After taking so many risks, to be turned in to her boss would be the worst. He might kill her. She stared into Robbie's brown eyes.

"Please don't betray us. Dan is getting some of the money too."

Robbie drove toward City Hall.

"What if Dan doesn't share his part with me?" Robbie said. "Then this'll be for nothing, and I'll leave with less than I started with. What kind of situation is that?"

"Just don't say anything to my boss."

Jas reached over and grabbed Andy's card, ripping it up into tiny pieces and throwing them out the window as Robbie turned right.

"There, now you can't call or text him."

"I memorized it, Jas. For heaven's sake, stop worrying so much. I won't call him."

Still, Jas wondered if she could trust this woman. Who was she? Was she really Dan's mother or were Dan and this woman pulling one over on them? How did they even know if Dew Drop Towing was a real company? She'd look it up online when she had time.

A siren blared behind them.

Flashing blue lights came from an unmarked police car.

"Pull over," an amplified voice said.

Jas massaged her temples. Not again. She should've looked around before tossing Andy's card.

Robbie scowled. "See what you got me into, throwing paper out the window?"

A police officer came over to the driver's side.

Robbie rolled the window down.

Jas wiped her moist hands on her thighs.

"Know why I stopped you?" a female officer said in a stern tone.

Jas turned away to hide her face in case Andy had circulated a photo.

Robbie said, "Because you like my car? I've been getting a lot of that lately."

"Your right blinker is broken. Driver's license and registration, please."

"Of course." Robbie dug in her big purse and in the glove compartment and handed over the documents. "I had no idea."

When the officer returned to the patrol car, Robbie said, "I didn't need this hassle with a traffic stop. All of this is your fault."

Jas gulped at the intensity of Robbie's anger aimed at her. But she wouldn't let this woman threaten her. She glared.

"You're the one with the bad blinker."

"And you don't have a car. Dan and I are the ones with wheels, so you'd better be grateful to us is all I can say. You owe us."

Jas said, "Dan wanted to come along, and we didn't invite you. You just showed up. No one owes anyone."

The officer returned, handing Robbie her license, registration, and a traffic ticket.

"Get your blinker fixed."

As Robbie put the car in gear, Jas sighed. Her best intentions to help her father had turned into a tangled web with too many people involved. Things were spiraling out of control.

26

BETS

Bets pulled long underwear on under her clothes. She turned up the heat in the house. The furnace roared to life, blowing hot air through ducts in the floor. Later today, she needed to change the natural gas bill to be in her name.

Zerk came out of the bathroom with a towel wrapped around his waist.

"Why's it so hot? I'm frying my fritters."

"I cranked up the heat. Why don't you make me a cup of tea to warm me up?"

As he worked in the kitchen, she peeked out through the gap in the tin foil covering the window. An eagle swooped down and snatched a fish from the channel. It flew away with flapping wings and perched on a branch in a tall evergreen tree.

Zerk set a mug on the counter with a clunk and rested a hand on her backside.

"What do you see? Anybody out there watching us?"

"An eagle."

Sitting on a stool, she wrapped her fingers around a cup

of steaming Red Rose tea. "We lucked out by ending up in this house."

He kissed her forehead. "That we did. I'll make breakfast."

While he cooked, she admired his biceps. Her mind wandered, and she drummed her fingers on the countertop, thinking about what they needed to do. He had to get his body art removed. Anyone searching for them would look for his dragon tattoo.

"Darling," she said, "where were you last night? Did you see anything interesting on your walk?"

He shrugged. "Just a little of this, a little of that."

He was being evasive and wouldn't meet her eyes, so she knew he was lying.

"I smelled cigarette smoke on your clothes when you got home."

He held up his hands. "I had to stop at the Brown. What could I do? The guys needed entertainment."

"You've already given the place a nickname?"

"Why not?" He hummed as he worked at the stove.

"In the future, just don't lie to me about where you're going. Is that understood?"

"Loud and clear, hon bun, loud and clear."

A few minutes later, he said, "Cheese omelets," setting a plate in front of her.

He joined her and as they ate, Bets smiled. Cheddar cheese, green onions, chili powder and black olives with green hot sauce. Thank goodness, the man could cook.

When they finished eating, she said, "Not to bring up a touchy subject, but you have got to get your tattoo removed. It's too obvious. We can't take the risk of someone recognizing you."

Zerk touched his neck, where the dragon's fiery red eyes

stared. The claws looked sharp as kitchen knives. The teeth were pointed.

He loved that tattoo, but it had to go.

With a sigh, he said, "I don't want to, but I should. I'll make an appointment."

While he did the dishes, because he was that kind of man, and she loved him for it, she showered and dressed.

At precisely ten o'clock in the morning, someone knocked on the door.

"Show time," Bets said.

Zerk opened the door to a young man with a buzz cut wearing glasses and carrying three boxes stacked on top of each other.

"I'm from Connectivity Plus," the young man said. "We offer customized solutions for each household's needs. I'm here to solve your tech problems."

The freshly-shaved kid looked in his mid-twenties, but it was hard to tell these days. Bets rubbed her cheek. The sun in Vegas hadn't done her skin any favors, and she needed to buy some face cream.

"Come in," Zerk said. "I hope this won't take too long. We've got places to go."

The technician smiled. "I'll have you up and running in no time."

Zerk pointed to the security camera they'd bought.

"We couldn't get this thing to work. That's part of why we called for help."

The tech put his boxes on the floor by the barstools. "Technology can frustrate the best of us. Let's see, you selected the Ultra Best Outdoor Security Camera that operates on battery power. Am I correct you picked this model so you wouldn't have to connect it to the internet?"

"That's right," Zerk said. "I wanted to keep it simple.

We're not computer experts. And I was worried about the data use and slowing down the Wi-Fi."

"Perfect points to consider when making a purchase like this. The good thing about the IP type security camera you purchased is it won't slow down your internet by taking up bandwidth. So, an excellent choice there. After I'm finished, you're going to have Wi-Fi, lots of bandwidth, and a security camera that connects to your phones."

"Sounds good," Zerk said with a smile.

Bets sat on a bar stool and studied the technician. Something about him was familiar, but she couldn't place it. Was it his voice? Who did he remind her of? When it didn't come to her, she shook it off.

"Nice view you've got," the technician said, glancing out the front door as he opened a box.

"I saw an eagle this morning," Bets said, chiming in, not wanting Zerk to do all the talking.

The technician hummed as he walked around the house setting up Wi-Fi.

When he approached the door to the small bedroom, Zerk stepped in front of him.

"No one goes in there except my wife and me."

"Understood. We all have our private spaces. Is it alright if I go into the basement?" the technician said. "I'd like to make sure you don't have any dead spots."

Zerk said, "Knock yourself out."

The young man went down to the basement.

A few minutes later, he came to the bottom of the stairs.

"You've got water in the basement. Did you know that?"

Bets looked at Zerk. Did the house leak, and Bill hadn't mentioned it?

"Looks like there's a sump pump down here, but the

switch is turned off. It rained hard last night. Want me to turn it on?"

Zerk said, "We'd better do that, so yes."

He turned to Bets with a question in his eyes. "Bill said to leave the sump pump on. Did you turn it off?"

She shrugged. "Mimi and I did, last night before you got home. It was too loud."

"Well, leave it on from now on," he said, frowning.

She nodded, thinking it was a good thing they balanced each other out. He was the practical one with cars and houses. Her strength was in anticipating danger.

Every now and then though, there was a hiccup. Like when she'd worn a hot pink blouse and red lipstick without a facemask to a job that attracted attention. The Dairy Queen cashier remembered them. They'd gotten away with only two-hundred-dollars, and they'd had to move cities. A big price to pay for a careless mistake.

"I didn't realize it was that important. I thought it was no big deal."

"I hope Bill won't charge us for water damage."

"It doesn't matter," she whispered. "We can afford it."

"We should go to the casino." His eyes lit up. "I'll win at blackjack."

She squinted at him to convey her displeasure. "We are not going to the casino and blowing the money like idiots. Remember the couple who sold their house and blew it all in Vegas in one night?"

"That's not us. We wouldn't do that. We know better, honey bunch."

She arched an eyebrow. "I'm not so sure."

The young man clomped up the steps.

The sump pump whined.

"See?" she said, throwing her hands in the air. "Like I said, it's loud."

Zerk cocked his head. "Leave it alone. Let it run. We can't have standing water in the basement. When it stops raining, it'll quiet down."

She turned to the young man. "Does it ever stop raining in these parts?"

The technician shrugged. "I'm not sure, I just relocated."

"Us too," Zerk said. "Where are you from?"

"Michigan, where we have lots of mosquitos, June bugs and poison ivy."

Bets cringed. How awful it would be to itch all over. Just the thought of it made her scratch the back of her hands.

The technician said, "We need to set up a network name for your Wi-Fi. What would you like to call it? Channelview? Or something else?"

"I like that," Bets said. "Sounds like a ritzy resort. Channel view."

The tech typed on a laptop. "Okay, there it is, and it's all one word with a capital c. Now for a password. We need one you haven't used before. How about oceansfour123?"

"Fine," Zerk said. "Whatever you think is best. We don't know anything about this stuff."

"You might want to write these down," the young man said, "in case you forget."

"I don't have a pen," Bets said. "Do you, hon?"

The technician whipped out a black pen and handed it to her.

"You can use this and keep it. Consider it a gift from Connectivity Plus."

Bets wrote down the information on her Safeway grocery receipt she'd stuffed into her jeans pocket that seemed like it was a mile long. "Okay, what's next?"

"I'll hook up a security camera that will connect to your phones."

Bets brought out the two phones they'd stolen from the would-be robbers the other night. "You look familiar. Have we met somewhere before?"

The tech stood still. His lips became a thin line.

Something about what she'd said bothered him. Why? She'd have to give it more thought.

"I don't believe so," he said, focusing on what he was doing.

Soon, the young man was walking out the door.

"I hope you'll give me a five-star rating if my company sends you a survey."

He was sincere, clean cut, and oozing youthful optimism. Boy, did he have a lot to learn about life. He had no idea about all the hurdles ahead.

Bets said, "Of course, we will." She waved goodbye, eager to see him go. The less time they spent talking with others, the lower the risk of being caught.

She closed the door and locked it.

Turning to Zerk, she said, "That kid looked familiar. I can't figure out where I know him from."

He shrugged.

"He's younger than us. Anyone that age starts to look alike after a while."

She tapped her chin, thinking. "I guess."

27

JAS

Back at Two Rivers Resort, Jas and Robbie put away the groceries. A frosty chill settled between them. What rankled Jas was how Dan's mother had invited herself along. Not only that, Robbie was giving off major attitude, saying Jas caused her to get a traffic ticket. Jas shook her head. There's no way a broken blinker was her fault.

Some people, like her boss, liked to blame anyone but themselves. Jas recalled the time she was in early at work going over a spreadsheet when Andy walked in, looked over her shoulder and saw revenues had decreased by ten percent in the last month.

"What?" he said, jabbing a finger at her, standing a few inches away. "You should've told me this earlier. Then I could've done something about it." His breath had reeked of stale coffee, and his lips had a dusting of powdered sugar from a doughnut.

He hovered over her, so Jas stood and opened the door to her office, which he had closed after coming in. She crossed her arms.

"I told you about the decrease in revenues. Last week. But you were playing solitaire on your computer."

"Next time, tell me when I'm not distracted or busy. Get my attention first, and tell me it's important. Tell me to stop what I'm doing."

She'd released a slow breath, amazed at his audacity. She'd told him about the change during their weekly meeting. She didn't sign on to be his mother or teach him when to pay attention.

"If you'll leave my office," she'd said, "I'll go back to finishing the report."

He walked past her.

"If your work continues to be sub-par, I'll have to replace you."

She closed the door and leaned against it, as if defending her office from invaders. In her last performance review, he'd given her an exceeds rating, which was the highest mark possible. She was fed up with working for an incompetent boss while, at the same time, worrying about her father's failing health. That event and the hallway slap on her behind triggered her decision to take advantage of the cash in the safe. She'd put it to better use than her boss's poker games.

Robbie's phone chimed, bringing her back to the present.

Jas pulled out her new phone and went outside to call her father from the front porch.

"When will you pick me up?" her dad said. "In two days, like you said?"

"I don't know if that's possible. I'll try. Things are difficult where I am, and I might be delayed."

Just then, Dan drove up.

He and Phil got out of the tow truck.

"Dad, I've got to go. Love you. See you soon, I hope."

As she pocketed the phone, Phil grinned at her. "I made it out alive."

Robbie appeared in the doorway. "Come in and tell us about it. I made lunch."

Sitting at the table eating peanut butter and jam sandwiches on white bread, Jas studied Phil and Dan's matching buzz cuts and horn-rimmed glasses.

"Nice haircuts, guys. You've got a retro vibe going."

Phil flashed a smile. He swallowed a last bite and took a sip of water.

"Here's what happened. I put a tracking device on their car before I went inside and left them with a spyware pen that'll record their conversations. What was weird was they had tinfoil covering the windows, so you couldn't look in or out. They've got two outdoor security cameras. One feeds to a memory card and the other to my phone, the one Zerk is using."

"Good to know," Jas said.

Phil said, "They were guarding a room, so that must be where the money is."

"Sounds like this'll be easy," Dan said.

Phil tilted his head. "I wish. In the basement, there's standing water down there. They turned off the sump pump and said it was too loud, despite the rain we had last night. I unlatched the basement door, so we can go in that way if we can't enter through the front. They rarely leave the house, for security reasons, which makes it harder for us to get inside."

Phil turned to Jas and Robbie. "What happened at City Hall? Did you find plans for the house?"

Robbie said, "Nope. They were all on coffee or lunch breaks." She rolled her eyes. "City workers."

"A man there," Jas said, "said to come back another time."

"That's fine," Phil said. "I was able to check out the place, we don't need those."

"But one problem did crop up," Jas said.

Robbie shot her a look. "Are you talking about my traffic ticket?"

"Not that. My boss is hanging around town. He walked over to Robbie's car and spoke with her. Offered her a reward if she'd tell him where I was." She clicked her fingernails on the table top. "I think he's serious, and he means to hurt us."

A murmur of concern came from the others.

Phil got up and returned with her purse. "I'd like to check and see if he put a tracking device in this."

She nodded. "Go ahead."

He unzipped it, rooted around in the black bag and said, "Ah hah."

He held up a round device the size of a quarter. "They're affordable for stalkers and cost under thirty-dollars. What shall we do with it?"

"Throw it down an outhouse?" Dan said with a shrug. "Except I don't see one here."

"Crush it under the tires," Jas said. "Grind it into the dirt."

Dan grinned. "I'll run it over with my truck. That'll do the trick."

He went outside and started the truck, backing it up and crushing the spyware.

Jas clapped. "Take that, you jerk."

Robbie and Phil cheered.

Coming inside, they sat and smiled at each other. When Phil took her hand, she squeezed his fingers. The next challenge of ripping off the robbers would be more difficult than stealing from her boss, but they'd do it as a team.

"We need to grab the money this afternoon," she said. "We'll get out of town before my boss finds us, so I can drive my dad to treatment in Mexico. After that, I'll have the rest of my life to do whatever I want, as long as I stay away from Nevada and this area."

"Which brings us to the money," Robbie said. "We're using my car and my son's truck. This morning, we had a little traffic stop thanks to Jas for calling attention to us when she littered. Bottom line is I want a quarter cut of the cash for taking part in this caper."

Jas, Phil and Dan were silent.

Jas clenched her jaw. Split four ways, she wouldn't have enough to help her father. He wouldn't have a chance at living longer. She wiped tears from her eyes.

Robbie said, "I'm part of this scheme, and I deserve a share. The money should be divided four ways. I deserve a cut for what I'm doing."

"Let's table that conversation for now," Phil said, "and talk about it later. Are we all agreed we're recovering the money this afternoon?"

"Yes," Jas, Dan and Robbie said in unison.

"Let's get it over with," Jas said, "before my boss finds us, or the robbers realize we're in town."

Phil glanced at his phone. "Zerk just searched for a tattoo removal place in Millersville. What do you think, Jas, if you pretended to do that? You could meet with him and distract him while we take the money."

Dan laughed. "Hate to say it, Phil, but that's the worst idea I've ever heard."

Jas said, "I'd need a disguise so the thieves and my boss wouldn't recognize me."

"I have an extra dress," Robbie said.

Jas nodded. A voluminous dress would be a distraction. "I'll wear the blond wig I picked up by the roadside. She might not recognize it."

She paused, considering what might go wrong.

"I'll tell you what, I'll wear the wig but skip the part about pretending to be a tattoo removal expert. If anyone runs into my boss, and he asks about me, please forget about the forty-thousand-dollar reward and lie to him. Say you saw someone with short brown hair getting on the ferry to Cedar Island. Or make something else up. Whatever you do, don't give us away. He's a vengeful man. He'll kill us if given the opportunity. He told me he killed a man for stealing his car, and he got away with it."

Phil stood up. "We've got a lot of planning to do before this afternoon. Let's take a break and meet back here in ten minutes."

28

BETS

Zerk pulled on his rain jacket and gave Bets a kiss. "I'll be back in a few hours, maybe longer. I'm going to get rid of my dragon tattoo." He touched his neck.

She moved Mimi off her lap and got up from the sofa.

"I know it means a lot to you. Hey, I'll drive you. You might be hurting afterwards and need a clear-headed driver. Besides, I need to get out of here."

"I don't know," he stuck his hands in his pockets and rocked from foot to foot.

"Okay, you don't want me coming along for some reason, I get it. Is it too much, not being able to talk to anyone else? Is that's what's getting to you?"

"That's it," he said, looking sheepish.

"Why don't you drop me off at the upholstery store I saw downtown, and I'll walk back. I need to get the couch cushion Mimi chewed on fixed or Bill and his mother will eat us for lunch."

She watched to see what he'd say. Was he having a case of the wandering eye again and wanted to be alone to check out women? The last time it happened, she'd shut it down. He and his fling never saw each other again. She knew, because she'd been keeping an eye on him.

It happened when they were hiding out after a job and living in a motel in Coos Bay, Oregon. When she wheeled a grocery cart out of a store, a woman in her thirties stopped her with a firm grip on her forearm.

"Your husband is messing around with my wife," she said, staring with cold, hard eyes. "And I won't put up with it."

Bets gasped. Zerk had promised three years before that he'd turned over a new leaf and was monogamous. Was the man capable of keeping it in his pants? Bets wondered how often he'd wandered since then. She was an idiot to believe he'd changed.

"I had no idea," Bets said, resting a hand on her acidic stomach. "I'll talk with him and make him stop. You'd better believe it."

The woman handed her a business card. She was a tarot card reader.

"Call me if you have trouble. Don't be a victim."

"I'm never a victim," Bets said, staring at the card. "And this is something I won't tolerate."

"Then we understand each other."

The woman tugged on her long braid and turned to go.

"Wait, what does your wife look like? Is she short and blond by chance?"

The woman's tweezed eyebrows went up. "How did you know?"

Bets felt like crying, but she pretended to be tough. That's what had carried her though life so far. Act like you don't care, and don't let them get to you.

"She fits his type," she said, tears clogging her throat.

The woman's stern face softened into a gentle smile. "If we can't make it through hardships, it was never meant for the long haul. Good day."

Now, Zerk cleared his throat. Old habits didn't die, so she'd have to watch him. He liked to be showered with attention, and she and Mimi often weren't enough to keep him occupied.

"Fine," he said. "I'll drop you off at the upholstery store."

She might be digging up dirt unnecessarily, but she wanted to issue a warning.

Shaking a finger, she said, "And don't you even think of hooking up with someone. That's all in the past, do we agree?"

He drew her into his arms and whispered in her ear. "You've got nothing to worry about, baby. I'm yours."

As Bets closed the front door, she said to the dog, "You be good this time. I'll be right back."

When Zerk dropped her off at Keen's Upholstery on Commercial, she carried in the mangled couch cushion. Presenting it to a woman at the counter, she said, "Do you think you can fix this and make it like new?"

"Let's see," the young woman put on her reading glasses and examined the rip in the fabric. Under that, Mimi had torn out a chunk of the cushion.

Bets pulled a piece of the foam cushion out of her pocket. "Will this help?"

The woman's laugh rang out like a bell. "No, but we can replace the foam and match the fabric. Hmm, it looks like this came from Bill's mother's house, is that right?"

Bets mouth dropped open at how small a town this was.

"Yes, that's where this came from."

"We upholstered it for her. I think we have some of the fabric still left. Let me check."

She disappeared and came back a few minutes later. Her eyes were so blue, she must be wearing contacts.

"We do have enough fabric left to cover the cushion. You're in luck."

Bets wiped her brow and hoped her lucky streak would continue. When their new house was finished, everything would settle down. But for now, she felt like the winds of change were howling.

The woman with the dazzling blue eyes wrote up the order.

"Thanks," Bets said as she walked out the door.

She paused in the doorway when she thought she recognized the person heading down the sidewalk toward the Brown Lantern. Was that Zerk? He was supposed to be at his cosmetic laser tattoo removal appointment.

She followed and ducked into a doorway when Zerk glanced back. Her heart thumped. If he was lying to her, she'd kill him.

A few minutes later, she looked out. He was gone. She slipped out of her hiding place and moved toward the pub, keeping to the shadows in case he came out of a shop.

Maybe he was buying a surprise gift for her. It could happen. Not likely, but possible.

Approaching the pub, a man came out.

Bets heard Zerk's hearty laughter inside. That was one thing he excelled at, being happy, and his high spirits usually carried her along. But that wasn't true now, not at this moment, not today when so much was at stake. She shook her head.

She stayed outside, sitting on a bench.

Through the window, she saw he was served a beer and headed back to the beer garden and smokers' area. She gritted her teeth. Hadn't he promised to give up smoking? Why did she bother to nag him when her efforts failed?

Bets went in and ordered a double scotch on the rocks. It was early, but she was ticked off and deserved it. She needed to calm her nerves before confronting him.

"Tough day?" the bartender said. She had sleeve tattoos down her arms, and Bets was sure Zerk had admired them. After all these years of being together, they knew each other well.

"Not really," Bets said as she paid in cash. "It's just that some days, even though everything seems to be going well, you get the feeling something's off. And it grates on you, you know?"

"I know all about that," she said. "Do you have a smaller bill to pay with? The customer before you paid with a fifty-dollar bill too."

She threw caution to the wind. This place would be her new second home. At least there'd be someone around other than Zerk to talk to. Every couple needed a breather from each other and a chance to hang out with other people.

"I don't, but you know what? Can I start a tab? Do you do that for frequent customers?"

"Sure, I can do that." Ms. Sleeves grabbed a pen and pad. "What's your name?"

She thought about what to say. If Zerk was going to be seen in public, she might as well be front and center too. "My name is Bets."

Ms. Sleeves held out a warm, firm hand, and they shook. "Hello new friend."

She sat there soaking in the wood paneling and tavern atmosphere for five minutes and then got bored. No one was sitting near her at the bar, and she was restless, so she ordered a second drink, knowing she probably shouldn't, especially so early in the day.

She took it to the back and found a perch near the door to the beer garden, where she could hear Zerk telling stories. The wood bench was hard, just like her heart. It was one thing for her to give her real name and have a drink. But for him to entertain three guys, from what she could see over her shoulder, when he should be getting the tattoo removed was too much. He broke the pact first.

"I've got another story like that," Zerk said, chuckling.

Bets rolled her eyes and stayed out of sight.

"Tell us about it," a man with a gravelly voice said.

"We were in Palm Springs, roaring up the main drag late at night when we see someone coming out of an art gallery and hauling away paintings. Now I knew that wasn't right. You don't shop at midnight for art, do you?"

Bets craned her neck and took a quick look.

"No, you don't," a short man wearing suspenders said.

A chill ran down her spine. Oh, my goodness. He's telling a story about us but pretending we were in a car driving by. When we were really the robbers. What is he thinking?

She took a sip of her drink. Her hand trembled, holding the glass.

"So right as we pull over to make a citizen's arrest, the guy drops the art on the sidewalk, hops into a waiting car with the engine running and the license plates blacked out. And they take off like bats out of hell. Woo wee, we couldn't catch up with them. Called it into the police, but they never caught 'em, far as we know."

Bets sloshed down the last of her scotch and drummed her fingers on the bench. Idiot. He was going to ruin everything.

"Hold on, guys, I'm going to get another drink. Anyone want anything? I'll pay for this round."

Zerk came in, and the screen door slapped shut.

Bets said, "Mr. Zerkowitz, we need to talk."

His eyes grew wide, and his hands dropped to his sides.

"What're you doing here, honey bun?"

"Forget the sweet talk," she said. "Sit yourself down right now."

When he did, she leaned over and whispered, "What were you doing out there, telling them what we did? You'll get us into trouble with the law."

"I changed it. We're the ones chasing the bad guys. No one will put it together."

He was defending himself, which riled her up and made her even more angry.

"All anyone's got to do," she said, "is look up Palm Springs art gallery robbery. These people aren't stupid."

"I don't think it matters. It's just a funny story to them. Now I need to get their beers and go back out there. They love me."

Bets groaned. There was no stopping him. He was a born showman and without an audience, he'd shrivel up and die.

"Why aren't you getting that tattoo off?"

He shrugged. "They canceled the appointment. Office had to close early for training or something."

She snorted. "Training? Sure, all of a sudden, with no notice. It'll be a long time until I trust you again. You watch out. The second honeymoon is over."

He stood and glanced out to the smoking area. "I'll see you at home."

"You bet you will."

29

JAS

Jas sat at Cabin Eight's kitchen table with the others. Before she and Phil robbed her boss, she'd been sure her plan would work. Naïve would be a better description, she thought as she chewed on a thumbnail. Now she knew better.

Lives were at stake. Andy was after her, and he had a track record of taking vengeance on thieves. If Bets and Zerk discovered where they were, they wouldn't hesitate to quiet them forever.

Her knees twitched under the table with adrenaline pumping through her.

"All right," she said, "we're going in this afternoon. Let's assign roles and responsibilities."

Phil said, "Excellent. We need someone to lure Bets and Zerk out of their house. Who's up for that?"

Robbie raised her hand. "I can do that."

"You'll be good at that," Jas said. "Make sure to lure them far enough away from the house so they won't notice us going in or coming out."

"Don't worry about me," Robbie said. "I'll pull my part off without a hitch. It's the rest of you I'm worried about."

"I'm worried too," Jas said. "We have to assume the money is in that room."

Her hands grew moist. The timeframe would be tight. "How long do you think you can keep them away, Robbie? Five or ten minutes?"

"Count on me for five minutes, but ten is pushing it," Robbie said. "If they're sticking close to the house, it'll be an effort to keep them outside for long."

Jas said, "We'll get in, get out and be invisible. We can do it."

"Robbie, we'll load the cash into your car," Phil said. "Will it fit? How much space do you have?"

"It might," Robbie said. "We'll have to see."

"She bought the GTC4Lusso," Dan said, "because it's got a back seat and cargo space. Never know what you'll need to haul around, right, Mom?"

The way he spoke and his mother's look made Jas suspicious. She picked at a cuticle. What if they threw the money in and took off? She had no idea who these people really were.

Robbie said, "True. But the V-12 is thirsty. I spent a ton on gas getting up here."

"What'd you get for mileage?" Dan said.

"Seventeen on the highway," Robbie said. "About what I expected from a high-performance engine."

Jas knocked her knuckles on the table. "Enough of the car talk."

Robbie's eyes bored into Jas. She said, "There's never too much of that."

"I agree," Dan said.

Jas leaned in to get their attention.

"Understood, and sorry if I offended you. Let's finish working on our plan. Robbie will create a distraction and draw them out of the house while Phil, Dan and I go in and take the money out. We'll go to Robbie's car, which will be parked out of sight on the street, and toss the money in the car as fast as we can."

Robbie gave her a sly smile, and Jas wondered if she could trust her. She swallowed hard. Her father was counting on her.

Jas said to Phil, "Which door will we use? The basement or the front door? I don't want to waste time hesitating or have crossed signals and be caught."

He drummed his fingers on the table. "The front door would be a straight shot out with no stairs, but it vastly increases the chances we'll be spotted. The basement door is better, because we can slip in the back unseen. The problem will be hauling money down the basement stairs and through the water. It'll take more time but be less visible. What do you think, Jas? We're doing this for your dad, so you get to call the shots."

The others nodded as Jas considered.

"Let's take the money out the front door," she said, "for a faster run at it unless we see them coming back. Robbie, can you whistle to us when you turn around and are heading back? That'll give us a chance to get out of there."

Robbie let out a warbling whistle, sounding like a bird. "How's that?"

"Excellent. We can't screw this up," Jas said, with a tremor in her voice. "I have to pick up my dad in two days and drive him to the clinic."

"Where's he going?" Robbie said.

Jas wiped her eyes. "Over the border in Mexico, near Tijuana."

Robbie said, "If this doesn't work, some of us might have to go with you."

Phil nodded. "We're almost done except for one detail. While we're in the house, how will we hear Robbie's whistle signaling they're heading back? We need a lookout."

Dan said, "I'll be the lookout until it's time to run to my mom's car. They don't know me."

"Good," Phil said. "And Jas, remember to wear the wig, so they won't recognize you."

30

BETS

When Zerk walked in the house, Bets stayed on the couch with Mimi. She didn't get up to greet him like she always did. She pretended to keep reading her Cosmopolitan magazine and acted her frostiest toward Zerk for telling the guys at the pub about their past exploits. Any robberies they'd done should be kept secret and not shared in any version with others. It was too risky to talk, as she'd told him time and time again.

He hung up his wet raincoat next to hers on a peg in the entryway, both coats dripping water on the floor. The sump pump went off and whined, providing the only sound since they weren't speaking with each other.

It was Mimi who broke the ice. She abandoned Bets and jumped off the couch, running to Zerk for a scratch under the chin.

"Traitor," Bets said, putting her magazine down.

"How long were you going to keep it up this time?" He glanced at a wall clock.

She couldn't help but smile. She loved this man so much

even though it didn't make sense. "I was going to keep you in the deep freeze all night."

He grinned. "You made it two minutes, baby, frosting me out. Longer than last time. Come on, let's dance."

He held out his hands and pulled her to her feet.

"I'm mad at you," she said. "I don't feel like dancing."

Wrapping his arms around her, he said softly in her ear, "But you love me, don't you? I love you, even when I'm being an idiot. And I know I was. I'm sorry."

He hummed to the droning monotonous tune of the sump pump as they slowly moved across the living room floor.

When they bumped into the coffee table, she said, "Let's take it into the kitchen. For a little more room."

Melting into his chest, she sighed. "Damn it, I don't want to love you, but I do."

"Me too, baby, me too." When he paused, she assumed he was about to say something romantic. Instead, he said, "It's odd, but I keep seeing a tow truck with Nevada license plates in town. Dew Drop Towing the sign says on the side. Why would someone drive a truck like that all the way here? Gas must've cost a fortune."

She'd hoped he'd been thinking about her, not tow trucks. "I have no idea."

Someone thumped on the door three times.

"Who would that be?" Bets said, her heart racing.

"Dunno," Zerk said with a shrug. "We'd better send them away."

"Alright, alright," she said. "We're coming."

31

JAS

Jas pulled Bets' blond wig on over her short hair with a knit hat on top as a disguise. The whole effect made her scalp hot. Sweat trickled down her arms. Her heart was racing like Robbie's fast car, and they hadn't even left Cabin Eight.

"We'll leave in ten minutes," Phil called out. "Do whatever you need to do to get ready. Meditation, stretching, visualizing."

"Get a life," Robbie said. "We don't need that crap."

"Don't knock it, Ma," Dan said. "I might try that stuff if I stop driving trucks."

"Whatever, it's your life."

Jas used the bathroom. Her knees were shaking. She strode outside to call her dad.

"Hey, pop, wish me luck."

"Good luck."

Her father's voice made her feel like she was ten years old, when all her hopes and dreams were possible. Her pulse slowed. A nearby bush rustled. She was riveted, watching for what made the noise. She didn't want to be discovered by her boss, not when they were so close to getting the money back and flooring it down the freeway.

"What's going on?" her father said.

"I'm going to get the money I promised you." She drew a shaky breath. "I just hope it goes well. If it doesn't, know that I love you and always have. You're the best Dad in the world."

"Honey," he said slowly, as if it pained him to speak. "You don't have to get that money for me. I'll enjoy the time I have left. Don't risk your life. Come back, and we'll go out dancing."

She snorted. There was no way he was strong enough to dance.

"I'll call you when it's over," she said, being stoic for her father's benefit. "I'll see you in a few days. Bye, Dad."

"Bye sweetheart. Take care of yourself."

When Jas hung up, she burst into tears.

Between sobs, she noticed a teenage boy running on a trail leading to the resort office. Must be the owner's kid, she thought. At this point, everyone was a potential threat until she was safely across the border with her father inside the clinic.

"Time to go," Phil said, clapping his hands.

They reviewed their plan one more time by Robbie's car before heading out.

Getting in the tow truck, Jas said, "Robbie's car is such a bright color. That yellow is certain to grab people's attention."

"That's exactly why she wanted it," Dan said. "She doesn't mind getting a little attention."

"I noticed," Jas said, hoping the trait of Dan's mom wouldn't be their undoing.

Dan parked the truck a block away from the house. They

put on hats and rain jackets to blend in with others on the street and gloves to avoid leaving fingerprints. A light drizzle fell as they approached Robbie's Ferrari.

Jas wondered how Dan's mom could afford such an expensive car. Was she on the up and up, or was she running scams? She gulped. What if she and Phil were about to be ripped off by Robbie and Dan?

But it was too late to turn back now. They had to get this done today, before they were fingered by her boss, or recognized by the robbers, and before her father's health declined further.

Phil motioned for them to crouch down near some bushes. He handed Jas and Dan wireless headphones he'd purchased at the electronics store. "Keep these on for communicating."

Jas put the headphones over her hat and wig.

"Testing," she whispered.

"One, two," Phil said, smiling at her.

"Three," Dan said, "that's me."

Jas smiled at Dan, glad he was along for his steadying force and sense of humor.

"As soon as they leave, we'll go in by the basement," Phil said.

Dan said. "My mom should be at the front door by now. Let's get closer to hear what she's saying."

"Come on," Jas said.

She led the men toward the thieves' house, her breath coming fast.

32

BETS

Bets and Zerk went to the door and stopped in their tracks. She held up an index finger and whispered, "Let's check our phones to see who's there, before we open the door."

A woman said, "Hello? Is anyone home?"

Bets checked the security camera feed on her phone. "It's an older woman."

"Wonder who she is?" he said.

Without waiting for an answer, he opened the door.

Bets groaned.

Mimi ran out, barking.

A plump, grandmother-type ignored the dog and gestured to the water.

"I'm so excited, I just have to tell someone." She smiled. "Whales are in the channel. I saw them over there. It's our first pod this year. If you hurry, you can see them."

Bets and Zerk hesitated and looked at each other.

Zerk said, "What'd you think, honey?"

Bets stepped outside, searching the water for whales.

This stranger was like a kind grandmother. Bets instantly trusted her.

"Sure, why not. Let's see what the real live Nature Planet channel has to offer."

The woman said, "The Orca whales are moving fast and going east, so we have to hurry. My name is Yolanda, by the way."

"Do you live around here?" Bets said.

"Just over there," Yolanda pointed in a vague direction. "I was walking by and saw them swimming past. Let's take this trail."

As Bets headed away from the house with Mimi at her heels, she had a vague feeling of unease. They shouldn't have trusted a stranger. They should've locked the house up if they left, even for a few minutes going down a trail. She shuddered.

Yolanda marched ahead, more agile than Bets thought a woman her age could move. "Almost there, just a bit farther."

Bets stopped. Panting from being out of shape, she had a sense they should return to the house. But she'd give it a little more time, because she did want to see what a whale looked like with her own eyes.

"Do you see them?" Bets said, breathing hard. Grandma Yolanda was a warrior woman who acted like she could run marathons.

"Right over there." Yolanda pointed and sure enough, Bets could see a whale spouting water in the channel.

Her heart skipped a beat at the beauty, and then she turned practical.

"I've seen enough, I'm going back. Thanks for showing us."

"Holy cow, that's a sight," Zerk said, staring at a whale. "Thanks for showing us."

Bets turned on the trail to go back to the house, but Yolanda reached out and snagged her arm with a firm grip. Bets blinked and gave the grandmother who smelled like lavender a good stare. What was she playing at? No one touched Bets like that and got away with it, not since her grade school days.

Yolanda pulled her hand away. "Sorry, I didn't mean to grab you so hard. My mistake. I only wanted to point out there's another one playing in the water, over there."

Bets glanced in the direction Yolanda was pointing and sure enough, two whales were surfacing and spouting water.

"Very cool, but I've got to go back. Urgent business. Good day."

"Me too," Zerk said. "You've seen two whales, you've seen 'em all."

"But," Yolanda said, sounding nervous and stepping in front of Bets and Zerk.

Mimi barked, as if she was trying to tell Bets something only a dog would know.

The woman said, "There might be more. A whole pod."

"I don't care," Bets said. "Get out of my way, you're blocking the trail."

Bets barged ahead. As they trooped back to the house, Yolanda followed behind, letting out a warbling bird-like whistle and repeating the call.

The sound was eerie and irritating. Even the dog didn't like it.

As Mimi yipped, Bets said, "Don't you have your own place to go to?"

"When I saw the whales, I parked my car and ran to see them. I'm going to my car."

Bets raised her eyebrows. Bets was starting not to believe Yolanda, even though she'd appeared trustworthy at first. One thing Bets had learned but forgotten just now with the knock on the door was to never trust anyone, not even your partner.

33

JAS

Jas, Phil, and Dan ran to the basement door. Phil opened it a crack. Robbie exclaimed about whales in a convincing manner, and Jas was impressed. When Bets and Zerk walked away with Robbie, Phil opened the basement door, and they stepped inside.

Water seeped into her golf shoes.

She could barely make out shapes in the dim light.

"I knew my mom could do it," Dan said. "She's a pro."

"What do you mean by that?" Jas said, beginning to suspect Robbie wasn't here to help them but to take advantage of the situation. Were they aligned with professional thieves? If so, she and Phil didn't have a chance.

She was a novice. After this heist, she was finished with crime. It was too big a hassle with a huge fear factor, keeping watch for who was out to get them next.

She crossed her fingers and hoped her boss wouldn't figure out where she was and come after her. If he did, what weapon would she use against him? Her wig? She was wholly unprepared for a life of intrigue and better suited to working in an office.

"Nothing," Dan said. "Just an expression. She's good at what she does is what I meant."

She sloshed through two inches of water in the basement and over to the steps. The Pacific Northwest paradise people talked about in her drought-stricken state wasn't as perfect as she'd been led to believe.

Phil led them up a flight of steps.

"Dan, go to the front door and see if they're coming back, or if you hear a bird whistle. Jas, help me carry the money out the front door. It'll be faster."

Dan moved to the open front door and listened.

Jas followed Phil into a bedroom.

Three blue trash cans were chained and padlocked.

Phil said, "This must be where our goldmine went."

Jas nodded. "I think it's safe to assume the money is in these." She added, as if the thieves were listening, "This is our money, and you can't have it. My dad needs it more than you do."

She grabbed the handle of a can and wheeled it out of the room.

Phil followed, grabbing a pen on the way out.

Dan stepped aside, nodding to them and looking serious, as they made their way to the yellow car.

The slight slope up to the street made Jas puff hard as she pulled the money up the hill.

"What's the pen for?" she said.

"It's a listening device. I wanted to hear what they've been saying."

When she tried to open Robbie's car door, her stomach dropped. "It's locked."

They ran around, trying the doors and the hatchback trunk, which didn't open.

"What was Robbie thinking?" Jas hissed.

"Maybe it auto-locked, and she took the keys with her by mistake."

"Oh, my," Jas said, trembling with fear. What had she gotten them into? This was too much, with too many opportunities for grave mistakes.

She pointed to the side of the road. "Let's hide the cans in the bushes over there."

Pulling the trash can, she raced to the bushes and shoved it among green leaves.

He set his can beside hers. "Let's go get the other one while we can."

They hurried to the house, went in the basement door, ran up the stairs and rolled out the last can. The wig itched. The hat and rain jacket made her hot. But none of that mattered. She had to grab the cash so she could help her father.

"Down the basement stairs," she said. "Less chance of them spotting us."

Phil went down the steps first, pulling while she pushed the can. She held onto the handle and bumped it down the steps. If it got away from her, it'd knock him down.

"Hurry," she said.

"I am."

His voice sounded tense, but she couldn't see his face with the lights off.

When the can came off the last step and rested on the basement floor, she bent over and caught her breath. Was it foolish to try and sneak off with the loot, when the two thieves were guarding it with their lives? Yes, but they couldn't walk away.

She knew it was twisted, but it was a matter of right and wrong. She stole the money, so it was hers. Or, hers to split with whomever she chose. Bets and Zerk shouldn't keep the cash when she'd risked her life and her job to steal it in the first place.

Phil hauled the trash can out the door.

"Come on," he said. "Don't freak out. Save it for later."

She snapped out of it and pushed the trash can up to the street. Had Robbie locked her car on purpose? Jas doubted it. But she was frustrated that Dan's mom made a mistake at a mission critical moment.

They rolled the trash can to the other two, which were behind bushes and under evergreen trees.

A red sports car with Nevada plates drove by and stopped at Robbie's yellow car.

Jas and Phil ducked behind the bushes, staying hidden from the street, or so she hoped.

The sleek red coupe reversed.

Jas reached out to Phil and wrapped her fingers around his for support. She sent her boss a message to look the other way. Keep going down the street.

When a bird's warbling whistle sounded, Jas looked at Phil.

How were they going to get out of here with the money?

34

BETS

Bets ran to the house, stumbling as she checked her phone for the video surveillance. Was someone taking their money? The kid from the resort might be stealing bourbon and tequila and hauling it away on his bike. Teenagers were idiots, always testing their limits.

On her phone, all she saw were trees. No people were trying to get in or wandering around the house. She let out a relieved sigh. They were safe.

Yolanda was a silly nitwit who liked making a bird-whistle sounds. Bets rubbed her forehead. Yolanda's bird calls were giving her a splitting headache.

"Zerk," she touched his hairy arm. "We don't need to rush. Everything's fine."

He bent over, breathing hard. "Good, I wasn't sure I could keep up with you. I've got to get to a gym."

She chuckled. "Every year you say that."

Yolanda rushed up to them. "Everything okay? You were in such a hurry back there."

"Just fine," Bets said. "I had an odd feeling and needed to

check on something. It's all good. Nice meeting you, goodbye."

Yolanda glanced at the house and turned toward the street. "Thanks for going with me. Everything's better when you have someone to share it with, isn't it?"

Bets and Zerk exchanged a look.

"Goodbye," Bets said, a hard edge to her voice. The woman didn't seem to be getting the message, and it was time to be stern. She had a nasty side, and she could turn on. Now was the time to use it.

Yolanda didn't move. She sniffed as tears trickled down her cheeks. "If only Bobby hadn't died so young. That's what devastated me and brought me to my knees." She wailed.

"Sorry to hear that," Bets said, glancing at Zerk. She'd been rude to a vulnerable older woman. She shouldn't have been rude.

Zerk said, "Would you like to come in? Bourbon might give you a boost."

Bets mouth dropped open. This wasn't what she wanted. He was far too friendly.

Yolanda blubbered. "My dear husband departed this earth much too soon, leaving me all alone. I'll never get over his loss."

Bets shot Zerk a look. They had to get rid of this widow.

He ignored her and took Yolanda's elbow, guiding her into the house.

"Right this way, it sounds very painful. We know just what you're going through. It takes the wind out of your sails, doesn't it?"

With a hiccup, Yolanda settled on a bar stool.

"Yes, it does. Thank you for understanding."

In the hubbub, Bets and Zerk left the front door open.

Zerk said, "Now Yolanda, what'll it be? Tequila straight up or Maker's Mark?"

"A wee dram of the Maker's Mark would be delightful," Yolanda said, dabbing her eyes.

When Zerk poured a finger's worth, Yolanda said, "Could you add just a little bit more? It's been such a hard day."

Zerk did that and glanced at Bets. "We'll have to get more, the way this is going."

Bets scolded herself for being heartless to a sad granny. Even she had a soft spot, although she didn't show it often. She went over and, as birds chirped and tweeted outside, she patted Yolanda's back. "I'm so sorry to hear about your husband."

"Oh, he wasn't my husband. He was my hamster."

Bets took her hand away and grabbed the tequila shot Zerk poured for her, downing it in one gulp. Was this woman crazy? Had they let a demented stranger into their house and relaxed their rigid rules for the wrong person?

"Just kidding," Yolanda giggled. "He was my husband, and I miss him so much. Could I have a bit more, dear? I don't want to inconvenience you, but I've got an awful burning in my throat. This'll take care of it, I'm sure."

Bets slid around the counter and poured a drop more for Yolanda, while helping herself to another shot. She was rattled by Yolanda's sitting with them. When the young technician left, they'd promised each other no more strangers in the house. Now that was tossed by the way side.

Yolanda glanced around.

"What a nice living room you have. It feels like home. I'd just love to lay down on that couch and let my cares drift away. I bet you two do that from time to time, don't you? Just relax and let the world go by outside with this beautiful view. But why do you have tinfoil on the windows? Don't you want to look out?"

"It's just an experiment," Bets said. "We'll take it down in a few days."

She gave her husband a look to keep quiet and not say anything on that subject.

Yolanda raised her almost empty glass.

"Shall we toast to each other? Oh dear, your glasses are empty. Let me fill them up for you. It's not right to pour your own drink, is it? Far better for someone to do it for you."

She poured several inches into two highball glasses and stopped, pointing out the open front door.

"Look, is that a great blue heron out there? What do you think?"

Bets and Zerk gazed outside, not seeing a bird or any wildlife at the moment.

"Guess we missed it," Zerk said.

With a shrug, Bets said, "I don't see anything."

Yolanda handed a glass with bourbon to Zerk and tequila to Bets. She hoisted her glass high and said, "To new friends."

Mimi barked.

Despite her earlier reservations, Bets found herself smiling at the kind grandmother. She lifted her drink before chugging it down to relax after a stressful day.

"To new friends. Even our dog likes you."

"Here, here," Zerk said.

35

JAS

The red car crept ahead, moving slowly down the street. Jas and Phil hid in the bushes. Dan jogged toward them.

He mumbled, "Where'd they go? Got to find them."

Jas stepped partway out of the bushes. "Over here."

Dan whipped around. "I couldn't find you. What happened?"

"Your mom's car is locked," Phil said. "We had to hide the money. Andy, Jas's boss, came by and stopped to look around, so we hid."

"I thought I was going to pee my pants," Jas said. "I was so scared."

"When I saw the chains, I went to my truck," Dan said, "and got the bolt cutters."

Dan cut the chains, and metal fell to the ground.

Just then, Robbie hurried to her car and unlocked it.

"Come on," Phil said. "Let's see what's going on."

They ran over and stood next to Robbie before she got in the car.

Jas's hands trembled. They had to get out of here before the thieves found them. Bets had a gun, and she'd use it.

Jas said in a low voice, "We need to put the money in your car. Where are the robbers?"

"I slipped a mickey in their drinks," Robbie said with a grin. "They're knocked out."

"Your car was locked," Phil said, sounding exasperated. "We couldn't load the money in it."

Robbie smacked her forehead. "I didn't mean to do that."

Or did she, Jas wondered. Had Robbie for some reason messed with their plans? She seemed to have it together too much to make a mistake like that.

A red low-slung sports car with Nevada plates rumbled up the street.

"Duck down," Jas said, gesturing to Phil and Dan. "It's my boss."

Dan crouched and said quietly, "That's a Porsche 911 Carrera coupe, costs over a hundred-thousand-dollars and goes from zero to sixty in four seconds. Always wanted one of those."

The sports car stopped and idled as a man got out.

Robbie pulled out a tube of lipstick and looked in the side mirror.

"Hello again. Did you happen to see the woman I'm looking for?"

Jas gritted her teeth. She'd know that entitled voice anywhere. Andy's dad had started the business, and his son never paid attention to the nuts and bolts of it. He was just interested in spending the proceeds.

"Not yet, I haven't." Robbie put the finishing touches on her lipstick and glanced at Andy's car.

"What brings you to town?" Andy said. "It's a long way from home."

"Sure is, but with a car like this, I wanted to take her for a longer ride. I might never go home."

Squatting by the car, Jas could see Robbie tapping a toe. Although she sounded calm, this had to be rattling her.

"I know what you mean," Andy said. "Is this where you're staying?"

Robbie shook her head. "Nope, just stopped to see whales going by in the channel. Nature's wonder, you know. That's a beautiful car you've got. How about we see how our cars do against each other on the open road?"

Jas shook her head. If Robbie took off, Andy might see them in his rear-view mirror. They'd be stranded without a way to transport the cash.

"It'd be an even match," Robbie said. "It's the driver that makes the difference."

Dan whispered, "Don't go."

"You know what?" Andy said. "You're on. Let's go up the hill to the viewpoint. First one there wins."

When Robbie jumped in her car, Andy took off like a shot.

The yellow car stayed where it was.

Robbie popped the back open and got out.

"Quick, before he comes back. Get the money in the car."

The four of them rolled the trash cans over to the car and one at a time dumped the banded and loose cash in the back.

Her pulse quickened. What if they didn't finish in time, and Andy came back and caught them? The lower half of the trash cans contained plastic bags with money. They tossed those in the car, working at a frenzied pace. Minutes ticked by. With four sets of hands helping, the trash cans were soon empty, rolling on the side of the road.

"I'm going with you," Jas said to Robbie, wanting to make sure she didn't drive off and take the money for herself.

Dan patted the car roof. "See you at Cabin Eight."

"Let's go," Phil said, "no time for goodbyes. Her boss will be back any minute."

Jas jumped in the passenger seat, making sure her blond wig and knit cap were on straight in case Andy stopped them. As Robbie roared away, the money in the backseat, some of which was loose bills, fluttered in the wind.

"Roll up the windows," Jas said. "We don't want money flying out of the car."

Robbie rolled up the windows and took a tight turn toward downtown.

Jas turned around, heart beating fast, and watched for a red Porsche coming up from behind.

"All clear for now. You were a genius back there."

"Thanks," Robbie said, focusing on the road.

36

BETS

Bets woke and rubbed her eyes. She elbowed her husband, who was sleeping next to her on the couch. Blinking at the open front door, she realized what had happened.

"Wake up," she said.

When he stirred and stretched, taking too long to understand the situation, she marched over to her purse to see what was taken. The only item missing was Jasmine's driver's license. Her body shook with anger.

Striding to her husband, she said, "Hand me your wallet. Let me look at it."

He pulled it out of his back pocket and gave it to her.

"What's going on?"

"I knew it," she said. "The grandma drugged us and took our driver's licenses."

"There's mine, right there."

He pointed to his photo ID in his wallet.

She was so angry they'd been tricked, her voice trembled.

"You idiot. The ones we were using for our new identities are gone."

He sat up straight. "The money."

As Bets ran to the small bedroom, she felt a breeze coming from the basement. Did the woman go out the basement door when she left?

Flinging open the door, Bets stopped and screamed. Instead of three plastic trash cans lined up in a row and secured with chains and locks, there were dust balls.

"No, not this," Zerk said, falling to his knees. "Anything but this."

She yelled, "How could someone do this to us? What happened?"

"It was ours," Zerk said, pounding a fist on the floor. "It was the culmination of our hard work. Our biggest heist is gone."

Bets felt her knees go weak. All her dreams had come true with the surprise money. They'd retired from robbing people and were living a new life.

Opening her arms, she yelled, "We've been robbed."

"What are we going to do?" Zerk said, staring at her.

She forced herself to calm down. They had to do something before it was too late.

"Hello?" A woman's voice came from the front door. "Anyone home?"

Bets put a reassuring hand on her husband's shoulder. "Take a moment to pull yourself together. I'll get rid of whoever it is."

She strode to living room, where Bill's mother was perched on the sofa next to the missing cushion. "I'm sorry Lucinda, but this isn't a good time."

She put on her frostiest face and please leave vibes, crossing her arms. Who took their money, and how were they going to get it back? Bets tugged on her hair and the pain made her feel better, distracting her from the twin problems: the missing trash cans of money and the builder's mom who had barged into their house.

Bill's mother pointed to the missing couch cushion.

"What happened to that? I don't want my things ruined."

Mimi barked and begged with her front paws up, in front of Bill's mother.

Bets sighed. "I'm sorry, but our dog chewed on a corner of it. The upholstery shop is replacing the cushion and the fabric."

Lucinda put a hand to her mouth, a hand holding two crisp twenty-dollar bills.

"I appreciate your doing that, but the fabric won't match. It'll look new."

Bets ignored the woman's minor concerns. The sight of the money made her fingers tingle. She wanted to reach out and snatch the bills from her hands.

Bill's mother held up the money, as if Mimi might chew the paper to pieces.

"I was coming by to see you and found these in the driveway. I figured it wouldn't be right to keep them. They must be yours?"

"Yes, they are, thanks," Bets said, taking the money and sticking it in her pocket.

Lucinda said, "You're awfully casual about handling cash. I'd be putting it in a dresser drawer or in the zipper pocket of my purse." She patted her tan handbag. "Hard to find anything in here, it's so big."

"Believe me, we are careful with our money. Just a minute, and let me call my husband in. He'll want to know about this."

Lucinda nodded. "Husbands like to be included about money issues, or at least mine did."

"Zerk," Bets called. "Can you come in here, please? Bill's mother found something you'll want to see."

Zerk lumbered out to the living room. His shoulders were down, his eyes were red and he looked sad. That made two of them. Bets felt like she could sit down and cry her heart out.

Bets pulled out the money, waving it in the air.

"Hon, look what Bill's mother found on the driveway. You must've dropped them when you were unloading the car."

A knock on the open front door made her turn.

A man walked in, smoothing his slicked-back dark hair.

"I believe that's my money. Where's the rest of it?"

He grabbed the money before she could tuck it in her pocket.

Bets wanted the money back and the man out of her house. She wasn't going to put up with bossy strangers who claimed something was theirs.

"Excuse me, but you're in my house, and you're not welcome," Bets said. "Now give me my money back and get out of here, back to whatever rock you crawled out from."

He didn't move or say anything.

"Who are you," Bets said, "and what are you doing here?"

The nerve, coming in her place and standing there like a stone. She'd toss him out so hard he wouldn't think of coming back. She waved her hand, shooing him out the door. This is what came from leaving the door open. And why hadn't the security camera beeped, warning her people were coming? Typical tech stuff, always breaking.

"Git," she said. "Go on, right out the door."

When she went over to him and started pushing him out the door, it was like trying to move a six-foot statue.

Suddenly, the man pulled out a gun and stuck it in her ribs, twisting her arm behind her back.

Her shoulder sent sparks of pain to her brain. "Let me go, that hurts."

"Hey, cut it out," Zerk said, trying to pull the man off her.

"I didn't come here to break up your little party. I only want to know where my money is. You have two of my missing items. Where's the rest? What'd you do with it?"

The man was breathing hard in Bets' ear, covering her in hamburger breath.

"Listen, buster," Bets said, pretending her arm wasn't killing her from the way he'd wrenched it back, "get over yourself. It was our loot. We didn't take it from you."

"Is that your car out there with Nevada plates?" he said.

"It is," Zerk said, stepping closer. "Let her go. What business is it of yours?"

"I'm from Nevada, and my company was robbed the other night. I'm here to recover what's mine." He shoved the gun into Bets's cheek. "See? I'm serious."

The cold metal barrel pushed into her face, and her mouth tasted metallic. She must've bitten her tongue. She refused to show him signs of weakness. "Nice try, but you're looking in the wrong place."

Zerk grabbed his arm and the gun, jerking it out of his hand.

Bets stomped on his foot while pulling away from the man.

As the gun hit the floor, a shot rang out with a flash of light.

The front window shattered.

Bets grabbed the gun and pointed it at the man, backing up toward her husband.

Lucinda stood up and went over to the bar stools. She lifted one up. "You think you can come in my house and wreck things? You have no manners. Go on, get out of here before I club you with this metal bar stool and call the police."

The man put his hands in the air and started inching toward the open door.

"There's been a misunderstanding. Money was stolen from my business outside of Vegas. Stacks of fives, tens, twenties, and fifty-dollar bills were taken from the safe."

"We didn't do it," Zerk said, holding a butcher knife from the kitchen. "I don't know who took it, but it wasn't us."

The man said, "I think my employee handed off the cash to someone else and that someone was you two. You thought you could get away with it. I want my money back."

Zerk's phone pinged, and he glanced at it.

"Someone's outside, the camera shows a man with a gray mustache."

He smiled, which to Bets was completely inappropriate considering the predicament they were in.

An older, broad-shouldered man in jeans came up to the front door.

"What do we have here? Zerk, you told me to stop by, but it looks like now isn't a good time."

He turned to go.

Bets's hands were sweaty on the gun. She held it up, aiming at the business man who had a tough-guy attitude.

"Harold," she said, "don't go. You might be able to help us with this situation."

He came back and stood on the front porch, lifting his ball cap.

"Harold Biggins, at your service."

Zerk said, "This guy accused us of taking his money. You can look around, but we don't have it. We've only got what's in my wallet and her purse."

"And her pocket," Lucinda said. "But now that's gone."

Harold nodded to Bill's mother and took his hat off.

"Pleasure to meet you. I met these two at Dad's Diner and spoke with Zerk at the Brown Lantern."

"My husband used to go there," Bill's mom said. "I only stopped by to say hello and came upon this situation. This rude man insists they have his money."

Bets aimed the gun, which was getting heavy. Her arms were shaking.

"Can we talk about what we're doing here?"

Harold said, "What would you like me to do?"

"Tie him up," Bill's mother said. "I've got rope in the basement."

Harold came back and, with Zerk's help, made the man sit on a barstool. They tied the man to the barstool, cinching it tight.

A breeze came through the missing front window.

Zerk covered the man's mouth with duct tape he'd found on the basement workbench. The man struggled and complained, but Harold knew his knots.

"Aren't you handy to have around," Lucinda said to Harold. "So strong and handsome."

"Just helping out," he said with a shrug, barely hiding a smile.

When Bets lowered the gun, Harold pulled out his phone.

"I'll call the police to report an intruder."

Bets panicked. She rested a hand on his muscular forearm.

"Please don't do that. We don't want the police coming here, do we honey?"

"No way," Zerk said.

Harold looked at the two of them. "Must be a story behind why you're saying that, but I'm not sure I want to know. Some secrets are best left unsaid."

Bets turned to Zerk. "Could I talk to you privately for a moment?"

They huddled in a corner of the living room, keeping their voices low.

Bets said, "We're out of money and back where we started the other night."

Zerk nodded. "Are you thinking what I am? Let's pack up and get out of here."

She kissed his warm lips. "Let's do it, before the cops get here."

They hurried to the master bedroom and packed their suitcases. She picked up her purse and went in the living room, with Mimi following.

"We're going to take off and say goodbye, Mr. Attitude over there. We didn't take your money, and you had no right busting in here with your gun."

She picked up the gun and wiped off her fingerprints with a dishrag, making quick work of it because she was a pro.

Setting the gun on the counter, she said, "We'll leave this behind so you can show the police. Harold, can you give us fifteen minutes head start before you call the cops? And thank you, Bill's mother, for providing us with a wonderful place to live for a few days while we were here."

Bets reached out and, in an uncharacteristic move, hugged Lucinda. Patting the woman's back, she smiled. She was turning into a real softie.

"I hope your insurance pays for the broken window," Zerk said. "It's this loser's fault."

Harold said, "I'll put a tarp over it so rain won't get in."

"My son will board it up with plywood," Lucinda said. "He takes good care of the place."

The man who was tied up tried to talk. He shifted from side to side and fell over, taking the barstool with him.

Zerk laughed. "Stay there like that and think about how it feels to have your house barged into. You scared the crap out of us."

"He was brandishing a gun," Lucinda said. "Can you believe it? In my home."

Bets stepped over the threshold and stopped to say, "You might also tell the cops to be on the look-out for an older woman named Yolanda. She's dangerous. She pretended to be our friend and stole our identification."

"Fake friends are the worst," Harold said.

They waved goodbye and as they walked away, Bets heard Harold say, "This is your house? Why would you move from a beautiful place like this?"

37

JAS

At Cabin Eight, Jas pulled a bedspread off a bed and used it to cover the cash in the back of Robbie's back seat.

Robbie came outside. "Must be boring, living out here. Too much fresh air for me."

"I'd be fine with it," Jas said with a contented sigh. "Hey, why aren't your car windows tinted? I thought all fancy sports cars had that."

"If Ferrari thought the windows should be tinted, they'd have done it at the factory," Robbie said, folding her arms like she knew best. "And if I have a car like this, I want people to see me driving it."

Jas nodded. If it was up to her, she wouldn't spend her money on a sleek car but on her dad and moving far away from Vegas, where Andy wouldn't find her. She glanced around, on the alert.

"I'll ride with you on the way back, all right?"

Something about Robbie's shift in posture gave Jas pause. A twitch of an eye and the way Robbie tightened her crossed arms made Jas wonder what was wrong. Robbie coughed and looked toward the resort office, which was a cabin re-purposed for check-in and a gift shop.

"Sure, that'll be fine."

"You've got to come see this," Phil said, standing in the doorway, his eyes wide, gesturing inside.

"Guess who's at Bets and Zerk's place? Your boss."

Jas cringed, knowing her boss could turn violent when he was angry. She didn't wish him on anyone, even her enemies. But at least he wasn't here, threatening them.

Phil pointed to his phone, where he had patched into the discreet security cameras he'd placed inside the thieves' house.

"What're they up to, do you think?"

Her heart fluttered, seeing her boss in the doorway pulling out a gun.

"Oh no, Andy has a gun. He's waving it around, but look at Bets, he grabbed her, and she's not scared at all."

"Give him hell, Bets," Robbie said.

Jas punched the air with her fist, wanting Bets to over-power her boss.

They watched as Bets spun around, out of Andy's grip, and Zerk grabbed his arm.

When the gun went off and the window exploded, Jas ducked, as if she was in the line of fire.

She found herself rooting for Bets and Zerk, who had a knife in his hands, and the older woman who looked huggable, the type you'd want to be your grandmother. If they stopped Andy, he wouldn't have a chance to hunt them down.

Phil said, "Who's the older woman? She's threatening your boss, Jas, with a barstool."

Jas cupped her hands. "Do something. Stop him."

Dan said, "Who's the older guy who just showed up? Anyone know him?"

"He looks mighty fine to me," Robbie said. "Oh, look, they've got a rope."

Dan chuckled. "They're tying your boss to a barstool."

"Tie him up," Jas said. "Tie him up."

"Make the knots tight," Phil said, as if he was coaching them. "I don't want him coming for us."

"Wait, what's going on now?" Dan said. "Bets and Zerk are leaving?"

"Looks like it," Jas said.

Phil shook his head. "They're taking their little dog and their suitcases."

"Hope they're not headed this way," Robbie said, turning to the stove and stirring a pot of canned chili. "Let's eat and get out of here."

"We could stay the night," Dan said. "Defend our turf and protect the car, if they come by."

Jas said, "I'm tired of running."

"Me too," Phil said. "I'm not cut out for a life of crime."

Robbie and Dan exchanged a look, but Jas wasn't sure what it meant.

Gulping down hot chili, her throat burned. Jas said, "Phil, can you see where Bets and Zerk are? From the tracker you put on their car?"

He scratched his chin. "What the heck? It shows the tracker is right outside."

They bolted for the door and looked around.

"They outfoxed me," Phil said. "They must've put the tracker on your car, Robbie, when you were with them seeing whales. Was there a moment one of them left for a minute and could've run to your car?"

"Anything's possible, I guess," Robbie said, running a

hand through her hair. "Zerk did disappear early on. He must've found it on his car. I thought he was taking a piss or something."

Jas said, her heart thundering, "We've got to get rid of that tracker. Where is it? I'll put it on that truck over there. Give it to me, and I'll take care of it."

Phil reached under Robbie's car, found the device, and handed it to Jas.

"Be careful, and be fast, my friend."

She hurried over to the South Island Septic Pumping truck, where a man was reeling in a large hose. A vague odor of an outhouse was in the air, so she breathed through her mouth.

"What a big truck you have," she said, leaning against it and putting the magnetized tracker on the metal under-carriage.

"Does the job and pays the bills," the man said, pulling off his orange rubber gloves. "Got to go, have a good day."

"You too, bye." Jas waved as the truck lumbered down the lane.

She jogged to the cabin.

"Mission accomplished. I hope they didn't check the tracker while we were here, with so much going on at their house."

"I still say we should sleep here tonight," Dan said, "and head out tomorrow."

Phil said, "Makes sense. Should we take shifts, watching the car, just in case?"

Robbie said, "I'll take the first shift. From ten to two."

"I'm exhausted." Jas yawned and stretched her arms. "I can't wait to hit that bed."

"I'll take the second shift," Phil said. "Jas, are you going to call your dad and tell him what happened?"

"I'm too tired now. My bones feel like they weigh a ton. I'll call him tomorrow when we're on the road, heading back to pick him up." She went to the bed and collapsed on the soft mattress. "Wake me up when I need to do something."

38

BETS

As the sun set, Bets drove their blue sedan out of town.

"Hon," she said, "why don't you check where the tracker is? Want to go get the money?"

Zerk looked at his phone. "It stopped at a wastewater sewage treatment plant. Wonder why that is?"

Bets laughed and smacked his arm. "Do you think they duped us? Could they have put it on a truck of some sort?"

Her husband nodded and started to chuckle.

"They got us back. The tracker's been at the sewage place for thirty minutes. Good one." He broke into peals of laughter.

"We've been had," Bets giggled. "Nice job, you youngsters. You'll learn new tricks yet."

"They weren't as green as we thought, were they?"

She smiled. "Not at all."

Patting his thigh as she drove, she said, "Now where shall we go? To a city or do you want to try living in Millersville? We could settle down and get jobs, work at a store or something."

He squeezed her hand. "Let try something new for a change and settle down. We can start over, can't we?"

She grinned and turned the car toward town.

"We can do anything we want from now on. No one will be chasing us. That man is locked up in jail."

"But we've got to tell Bill we can't build the house."

She nodded. "We've been in tough situations before. We can handle this."

39

———

JAS

Jas felt a hand on her shoulder, shaking her awake. She opened her eyes in the pitch dark.

"Wake up," Phil whispered.

"What time is it?" she said.

"Robbie left."

Jas sat up in bed. Her stomach soured. If Robbie left, it meant she'd taken the money, neatly packed into her car. Jas wouldn't be able to help her father.

"Are you sure?"

He took her hand and guided her outside. The cool, moist air was a shock, after being warm wearing her long underwear in bed. A light from a pole near the office shone.

The yellow Ferrari was gone.

Her throat closed with tears. What was she going to do now? She had no job, she had no money, she had no way to pay for her dad's medical care. He wouldn't get a chance to live longer.

Tears streamed down her cheeks. "We went through all this for nothing? We trusted her and while we slept, she took it and ditched us?"

Phil held her hand. "I've felt more alive in the last few days than I ever have. And it's all because you asked me to join you on this risky adventure."

She wiped her eyes. She'd have to find a way to break it to her father, with loads of tissues on hand because she'd be the one crying her eyes out.

"A foolhardy heist, it turned out to be. I never thought we'd be empty-handed after chasing them down and escaping with the money. I have to tell my dad I disappointed him in person. Will you come with me?"

He squeezed her hand. "I'd love to join you on another trip. But this time, we won't rob anyone. We'll just have to move somewhere they don't know us."

The lights came on in the cabin.

"Guys?" Dan stood in the doorway in his boxer shorts. He was smiling. "I think you'll want to see this."

On the table were stacks of money. In a separate group on the floor by the kitchen sink were more.

"I'm glad she left us some of the money," Jas said, breathing a sigh of relief.

Phil said, "Why are they on the table and on the floor?"

Dan tapped the table. "Read the note."

On a crumpled piece of paper, a handwritten note said, 'I sent Dan an email. Have him read it to you.'

Dan checked his emails.

"Here's the one. Want me to read it out loud?"

"Yes," Jas said, throwing on her awful purple skort and pink polo shirt over her long johns. She couldn't wait to ditch these stinking clothes and buy something that suited her better. Just a pair of jeans and a t-shirt would work. She'd never wear a skort again, no matter what.

Dan said, "Okay, here goes."

He raised his voice to a higher pitch so he sounded like Robbie.

"Didn't want to say goodbye in person. The road called, and I had to get going before dawn. Nothing like night-driving in a high-performance car, purring along and having the highway to myself. I took thirty thou for my part, since I joined you late, set aside the money for your dad, Jas, and split the rest between you three, which means you get ninety thou each. Jas, I hope your dad gets better. Dan, I'm taking your part back to Vegas, since your truck will be crowded with the three of you and the money. I'll see you back in Vegas when you find time to stop in. Phil, may you laugh and be happy. Keep being brilliant and humble. You're a talented young man, and you saved the day. If you ever want a job acting, call me. Fly free and be mighty, Robbie."

Jas turned to Dan. "She mentioned acting. Is she not your real mother?"

He shook his head, looking sheepish.

"Sorry, guys. She runs an acting school I've been attending. She coaches famous actors and pulls in the cash. I've been thinking about branching out. Thought I'd learn how to be entertaining and convincing."

Phil made a fist and tapped Dan's shoulder.

"You old dog, you. Tricking us like that."

Jas laughed. "He did. I totally believed your act. But what about the stories you told when we first met you? About your mom and the ranch?"

Dan grinned and looked proud of himself.

"I was trying to scare you and trying on a role. It worked, didn't it?"

Jas looked at Phil, who nodded.

She said, "You definitely convinced us."

Phil tapped his stubbled chin. "But when did you bring Robbie into it?"

Dan said, "To tell you the truth, I was thinking of it as improv theatre. And I thought we needed a mother figure to round out our group. Robbie's smart, and I thought she'd increase our chances of getting your money back."

Jas hugged Dan. "Thanks for your help. It was crazy, but it worked. Why don't we get going, since we're awake?"

"We'll stop at a Starbucks," Phil said. "There has to be one between here and Seattle."

"Hate to break it to you," Dan said, "but it's too early for them to be open."

They put the money in trash bags and moved them to the truck cab.

Dan patted the truck before he got in.

"I love my Ford F-650. She's a sweet ride."

Sitting between the men as they drove away, Jas said, "I wonder where Bets and Zerk are now?"

40
______

BETS

A week later, Bets sat in the yard of a little house they'd rented on the edge of town, drinking tequila on ice and looking at the local paper's police blotter. Sweet-talking the landlord and promising to do maintenance and repairs had swung the lease in their favor.

Zerk sat next to her in a matching lawn chair. "Ahh, this is the life, isn't it, hon? We're working at the Brown Lantern, and we're going straight."

"You'll be the best bartender they've ever had," she said with a smile. "Except for me, of course. We'll add zest to the place, with our sparkling personalities."

"Now that the money's gone, we can make friends."

A flicker of concern crossed her face. "I hope we'll find people with a spark to them."

"We'll find like souls, I'm sure of it." He sipped his drink. "Bill was sure ticked off about our not building the place. But we didn't have a signed contract."

She lifted her hands. "What could we do? It's not our fault we got ripped off."

"I'll take him out for a drink to smooth things over."

Bets pointed a manicured fingernail at the paper.

"Look at this. Las Vegas man released from Millersville jail. No evidence found against him."

She crumpled the paper and threw it across the grass.

"How could they say that?" Zerk wiggled a finger in his ear, which he did when he was confused. "He was ready to shoot you."

She scowled. "Maybe he had an in with the cops. Or greased the wheels. Not like with us normal people."

"Honey buns," he said with a smile, "we'll never be normal."

They laughed, and Mimi the dog yipped.

41

JAS

Jas drove Phil's car across the border into Mexico, with her father in the front seat and Phil riding in the back. The car had been found in a motel parking lot. The police told Phil they thought it had been kids joy riding. Jas avoided going with Phil to the police station. It was best if they didn't know she was in the state, picking up her father.

In the trunk were the second set of books she'd taken from her boss. If he managed to find her, she'd turn him in to the authorities. They'd left some money in Scottsdale, dividing it between a bank's safe deposit box and a home safe installed in Jasmine's father's house. Phil was handy like that.

Her dad smiled. "I appreciate all you two did, taking out a loan so I can go to this place."

Jas winked at Phil in the rear-view window. "I want you to get the best care possible. I love you, and you deserve it."

The sun shone bright, blazing in the car windows, as Jas drove up to the medical center on the outskirts of Tijuana. It looked more like a wealthy person's mansion than a facility that might help her father improve his health.

"Remember," she said, wagging a finger. "Do whatever they say. And call me to let me know how it's going. We'll be staying in Sayulita while you're here."

"You'll be at the beach while I'm being treated. Can we switch places?"

Her father's laughter turned into a coughing fit that tore at Jasmine's heart.

"No funny business from now on," she said, patting his hand. "I'll make the jokes and do the laughing for you until you get better."

When he'd checked into the facility, Jas hugged her father goodbye.

"We'll come see you on Sundays. Just be good until then."

He hugged her hard, with more strength than she'd realized he had.

"Bye, pops. Be good and get well."

She kissed his cheek, and he held onto her arm, as if he didn't want to part either.

"See you Sunday."

Jas turned and threw her father a kiss.

Taking Phil's hand, they went outside.

"Ready for a vacation?" Phil said.

"Yes, it's been the longest week of my life."

"One more thing," he said, stopping at the car. "How about a kiss?"

She wrapped her arms around his neck and let her mouth linger on his soft lips.

This was going to be a very good vacation, she suspected. The best she'd ever had, if she was to guess.

Maybe they'd move to Mexico. Who knew what the future might hold?

Thank you for reading this! Please let other readers know what to expect by posting reviews on Goodreads, Amazon and Bookbub.

If you enjoyed The Thieves, then sign up at www.susanspechtoram.com.for my newsletter to be the first to hear about my other books.

Check out my next book in the series, Cabin Eight. She's used to cleaning houses and getting down in the grime. But the dirt she just dug up could kill.

Find me on my Facebook author page

Follow me on BookBub for the latest updates!

ACKNOWLEDGMENTS

I'm deeply grateful to Sue Toth for her developmental editor insights. A huge thanks to Rick Dahms of Rick Dahms Photography for the professional headshot. Thanks to Bill Isenberger at Axis Studios in Seattle for his website expertise for: www.susanspechtoram.com.

Thanks to the Pacific Northwest Writers' Association. Many thanks to the Women's Fiction Writers Association for support and information. Most of all, thank you to my parents, Liz and Ed, to my children, Nick and Forrest, and to my husband Jerry, for making me laugh.

ABOUT THE AUTHOR

Susan is writing mysteries, thrillers, and suspense novels. Previously, she served as senior director of corporate communications for biotechnology companies. Susan worked as an activity aide in an upscale nursing home's psychiatric unit. She was a potter and painter with an art studio in Seattle and has also been a market researcher, a nurse's aide, a waitress, and a library page. Her essays have been published in Mothering Magazine, Twins Magazine and Utne Reader.

Susan grew up near Detroit, Michigan and received a BFA with Honors from University of Oregon and a MBA in Marketing from Seattle University. She lives in a windy part of the Pacific Northwest with her husband and their rescue dog.

BOOKS BY SUSAN SPECHT ORAM

Shore Lodge

The Thieves

Cabin Eight

The Mother's Threat

Secrets at the Cafe

Under Jackson Bridge

Humorous fiction:

Boating with Buddy, a report from a canine correspondent

Nonfiction:

Brief business books on investor relations, crisis communication
and public relations